All Angela really wanted was to wrap her arms around him.

But she willed herself not to move, struggling to remember all the reasons she should leave Ricardo alone. He considered her teaching methods ineffectual, her classroom chaotic, and his news story had the potential to harm her and her programme. But her desire overruled every argument and when Ricardo gathered her into his powerful arms, she went willingly.

With ease, he braced her against his chest. "Let me hold you for a few minutes."

It felt so right to be held by him, and she closed her eyes as waves of arousal rocked her. Then she pulled away.

"*Querida*," Ricardo said huskily, "we could make love now. We both want to, don't we?"

Her body ached with longing, yet she hesitated. "But where would that lead us?"

To my in-laws, Ed and Flo Smith,
who can give us all lessons in love.
Happy 50th anniversary.

———— ✿ ————

SANDRA LEE
is also the author
of this novel in
Temptation

OVER THE RAINBOW

Love Lessons

SANDRA LEE

MILLS & BOON LIMITED
ETON HOUSE, 18-24 PARADISE ROAD
RICHMOND, SURREY TW9 1SR

First published in Great Britain in 1992
by Mills & Boon Limited, Eton House, 18-24 Paradise Road,
Richmond, Surrey TW9 1SR

© Sandra Lee Smith 1992

ISBN 0 263 77995 5

21 - 9211

Made and printed in Great Britain

1

"WHAT TIME DID I SAY he was coming?" For the umpteenth time that morning, Angela Stuart nervously pushed a loose strand of her blond hair away from her face.

"Nine o'clock." Maria, her close friend who had team-taught with her for years, sighed with impatience. "Why are you so nervous? Nearly every week you have visitors in your classroom, and usually you're so composed."

"This isn't the same." Angela took a deep breath, trying to settle the butterflies in her stomach. "They come to observe how I teach. Ricardo de la Cruz is coming to criticize."

"So?" Maria waved her hands. "You've never let a little criticism bother you before."

"I'm really concerned this time, though, that I won't be able to defend the program against his criticism—no matter what I say—because I've heard he's dead set against it. The whole-language approach puts people off at first because it's so different from the older, more structured methods. Yet, once people understand the theory and witness the fantastic effects on students' motivation and progress, they're very supportive."

Angela walked over to her desk and again straightened the stack of first-graders' papers.

"Don't you think de la Cruz is going to recognize these things?" Maria asked.

"It takes time to understand. At first glance the classroom looks chaotic. What if that's all he sees? What if he doesn't look below the surface?"

"You're worrying needlessly. What can he do?" Maria reasoned.

"But Ricardo de la Cruz can affect my program ... my job, even." Angela paused.

Although Ricardo was no longer on the board of the Valley of the Sun District School Board, as a star television-news reporter, he had considerable power and influence. His strong interest in Phoenix's education policy was renowned. He'd made a point of being involved—by sitting on school boards and regularly covering stories on education.

Of course, his charismatic personality also contributed to high visibility. Angela had watched him perform—yes *perform* was the word to use—at the board meetings, where he exhibited the same intelligence, drive and fervor that made him such a popular reporter.

"Since he's no longer on the board, what can he do?" Maria asked.

"He's an investigative reporter. What if he digs up facts about my past?"

The district school board knew about her first teaching job and why she'd left, but the thought of the scandal being splashed across the television screen made her stomach quiver.

"You know for a fact that even teachers who've observed the approach being used in a classroom still don't believe that first-graders can read books, research and write their own stories. They're skeptical because of the radical changes in thinking they'd have to undertake."

"You mean Lupe Cartegena and Cathy Jones."

"Exactly." Those two teachers were so sure the traditional way was right that they refused to even consider trying the whole-language approach, and there was a very real possibility that Ricardo de la Cruz would respond the same way.

"He's relentless, Maria. If he decides he doesn't like the way I teach, he'll make it very difficult for me."

"He's only here as an interested resident and taxpayer. He has a right to observe what's going on," Maria reminded her.

"But why my room? Why not yours or Mike Garrett's?"

"You handle visitors and explain the whole-language approach better than we do. The way you relate the learning of reading and writing to how we learn to speak makes so much sense."

"The process is so powerful. Everyone has the ability to communicate, no matter what language or culture they're born into. If you teach reading and writing the same way you instinctively teach your child to talk, every child will succeed."

"See what I mean?" Maria said.

Angela tucked in the strand of hair that started to fall from her chignon. "I suppose you're right. I'm just edgy—you should have seen how Mrs. Edwards summoned me to the office and told me he was coming to check me out."

"When he sees what a great teacher you are, there'll be no question about your job," Maria reassured her friend, confidence showing in her dark eyes. "This isn't Yuma. You aren't going to be fired like you were there."

Angela shuddered at the memory. "You don't want to imagine what it was like to be ostracized like that."

"Like you always tell me—think positively. Besides, you have the backing of the professors from ASU."

"That won't do me any good. You know what the administrators think of *them*." The Arizona State University professors she worked with were internationally renowned in their field, but that didn't impress her district office personnel. "They think Dr. Wheeler and the others are only after research data—not the improvement of schools."

Maria shrugged. "That's because of what's happened in the past. Seven years ago, another team from ASU came to our school, used the kids as guinea pigs and then left. We never heard from them again. No results—no conclusions."

"But that's not the case with us. Our findings are changing education. Look at all the successful teacher workshops we've held. We keep getting requests from other states to share our findings. If de la Cruz gives our project the ax, we lose all our credibility."

"You're getting upset about something that hasn't happened," Maria pointed out. "Prove to him that your methods are effective. He's known for his honesty."

"You're right." Angela paced and stopped in front of a brightly colored display of her students' work. Stories and pictures about each of their families were mounted on the wall. She read their descriptions and felt a measure of confidence return. Her students excelled because of her implementation of the whole-language program. Nothing could refute that fact. If Ricardo de la Cruz tried to discredit it, she would fight back.

"I'll be fine." Angela braced her shoulders.

"Thatta girl." Maria laughed, relief showing in her face. "The bell's going to ring in a few minutes. I'll go pick up the kids."

Angela watched Maria disappear down the corridor toward the playground. A noise from the connecting door to Maria's classroom caught her attention. She turned and stared.

Ricardo de la Cruz stood in the doorway. Wavy brown hair set off chiseled Hispanic features. His black eyes flashed with self-confidence and challenge.

"Morning," he said.

Before Angela could respond she heard a mumble and movement behind the tall reporter. He shifted slightly while the principal, Mrs. Edwards, bustled into the room.

"Mr. de la Cruz," Mrs. Edwards trilled in her high-pitched voice. "This is Miss Stuart, the teacher of our first-grade bilingual class."

It amused Angela to see that in spite of the fact that Pamela Edwards was an active member of several legislative committees, the principal was in the same flustered state as herself. De la Cruz strolled toward her and Angela felt every nerve flash a red alert.

"We've never been formally introduced, but I've seen you at the board meetings," he said, smiling, and then greeted her formally. *"Con mucho gusto, profesora."*

Angela took his outstretched hand and tried to speak. The Spanish that she'd studied so hard seemed to jam in her throat. All she could focus on were the sensations racing through her fingertips.

Finally he broke the silence. "Why, thank you. I'd be glad to make myself at home in your classroom."

Angela quickly glanced into his eyes and noticed amusement there. The nerve of the man! How dare he come to criticize, and then laugh at her nervous state? Angela quickly shifted into gear.

"I know why you're here, Mr. de la Cruz." Good. She sounded assertive. It wouldn't help her cause for him to know how anxious she was. "All I ask is that you keep an open mind and carefully observe the performance of my students."

"I came to observe *you*."

"By observing the students' performance, you'll be able to judge my effectiveness," she countered.

"It's difficult to understand how a teacher who doesn't use textbooks, who doesn't maintain an orderly classroom and—" he paused to look meaningfully around the room "—doesn't follow prescribed teaching methods can be effective."

Angela felt her heart sink. Apparently he'd already made up his mind. Just then the door opened and her students filed in with their eager smiles of greeting. When Angela saw their expressions change to wary regard upon spying Ricardo de la Cruz, her defenses rose. The children responded intuitively to any new situation and would sense the tension between their teacher and this stranger; she wouldn't allow that—even if he was a reporter.

"We'll discuss this later," she told him. "For now, please simply observe."

He bowed slightly as she walked past him to greet her class. She automatically proceeded with the morning routine while her mind focused on her visitor. Mrs. Edwards was guiding him around the room and explaining, no doubt, what all the unusual exhibits consisted of. She hoped he'd be astute enough to recognize the educational implications of what was there.

Ricardo was staring at the classwork, but he wasn't seeing it. His attention was focused on Angela Stuart. All of a sudden he hated this self-imposed assignment. He wanted out of it. But that would be shirking his responsibilities, and in his thirty-two years, he'd *never* done that. But here he stood—wanting to turn around and walk out of this room.

Why? He knew the answer. Angela Stuart intrigued him—and not for the first time, either. At each board meeting she'd attended, she'd been distracting him more and more. It wasn't just her beauty; it was her warmth and intelligence. He shifted away from the wall and glanced at her. She stared back with a hint of challenge.

He looked away. After he finished this investigation she might not give him the time of day, let alone allow him close.

He eased his way around the desks as he followed Mrs. Edwards to another display. He recalled the anonymous letters he'd received. *Angela Stuart, a teacher in the district for five years, is incompetent. Angela Stuart does not teach her students. She never uses district textbooks or other standard methods of teaching. Angela Stuart's classroom is out of control— the students run wild.*

He was no longer a member of the school board but he still attended meetings and was actively involved. When the letters had arrived, he'd felt compelled to check up on them. Now that he was here, he wished he'd dumped the problem in someone else's lap.

He shook his head. The accusations didn't seem to fit the woman he saw in front of this class. But if she proved to be incompetent, she'd be out.

"What a pity," he murmured aloud as he listened to her clear soprano. She led the class in singing "America," her voice mingling with those of her students.

"I beg your pardon," Mrs. Edwards piped up beside him.

"She sings well," he said.

"She puts on a wonderful program every spring," Mrs. Edwards said enthusiastically. "The parents really look forward to it."

Ricardo nodded, focusing his attention on Angela.

"She does a lot with the parents," the principal continued. "She holds workshops every week and instructs them on how to teach their children at home."

"All her effort and enthusiasm are highly commendable," Ricardo agreed. "However, I still question her teaching methods."

Ricardo rocked back on his heels and studied Mrs. Edwards. Angela certainly had the woman's support and apparently that of some of the parents.

He could see why. She could charm with that smile. The letters he had received said her class was unruly, but watching her with her students, he had to admit she had them in the palm of her hand. But not him. He was tough. You had to be, to travel the road from poverty to news reporter for KSTR. No, her charm wouldn't sway him. The evidence—and only the evidence— would be considered if he had to recommend she be relieved of her teaching position.

Suddenly the door opened and a small boy entered and ran over to Angela's side. His black hair fluttered in his eyes as he apologized in rapid-fire Spanish for being late.

"*Está bien.* It's all right, Juan." Angela smiled and gently brushed back his hair.

The boy held out his hand. Ricardo could see the pride in his face as he offered a flower to Angela. But when he saw its broken stem and wilted petals, he looked crushed. Ricardo wanted to reach out to him, but Angela did, instead. She accepted the gift as if it were the greatest treasure on earth.

"*Gracias.* Thank you," she murmured while she draped her arm across his shoulders to give him a quick hug.

Ricardo's heart filled with emotion. *¡Caramba!* He silently swore. This woman's compassion was distracting him from doing his job. If she was an incompetent teacher—then he would prove it. Wasn't that why he'd run for the school board five years ago? To make Valley of the Sun district one of the best in the state? And if that meant firing teachers, he'd see to it. The fact he was no longer a board member wouldn't deter him in the least. Board members still valued his opinions, and if need be, they would seriously evaluate any report he gave them on Angela Stuart's teaching methods.

Ricardo positioned himself on the corner of a table, suddenly recalling the poor excuse for a school he'd attended in the barrio of East Los Angeles. He welcomed the anger that began to simmer inside him as he remembered his difficult youth. It helped to remind him of his purpose. The students in *this* district would have quality education. Living in a barrio in the inner city wouldn't be the handicap to them that it had been for him.

"We have a special visitor today, class. Mr. de la Cruz has come to see how good you are."

Clever psychology, he thought as he waved a greeting to the eager students. He could see some of them itching to show off their skills.

"What languages do you speak, Mr. de la Cruz?" Angela surprised him by asking.

"English, of course." He hesitated. "And Spanish."

To his amazement, the students clapped their hands. "He's bilingual like us, teacher!" a boy called out.

As he scanned their faces, Ricardo saw the children's pride in their heritage and language. Was she responsible? It seemed unlikely. What would *she* know about Chicano pride?

"Since he understands both, you may read your stories to him in Spanish or English," she went on to direct her students.

What did *that* mean? Surely she wasn't going to have him lead the reading groups. He could have saved himself the worry. As soon as she reminded the students that they were all at school to work and learn, they stood and hurried to various workstations in the room. Ricardo had to step back from the onslaught of running children.

Shocked, he looked over to the principal and then at Angela. Neither one seemed the least bit concerned. *The letters had been correct. She had no control of the class.*

Didn't she care? Why didn't she do something? He wanted to walk over and shake her—to tell her to control her class so that he wouldn't have to turn in this report.

"Mr. de la Cruz." The high-pitched voice of a child caught his attention. A tiny hand reached up for his and tugged. "Wanna hear my story?"

"Sure, *mijita*." He followed the tiny girl with the swinging pigtails into a corner of the room. She pulled him down onto a pile of pillows. Good. Now he could watch Angela while seeming to focus on the child.

The girl appeared to be no more than five years old, yet she read well, and with confidence. Ricardo listened with growing interest.

Must be "the brain" of the class, he thought. But to his surprise, other students joined them on the pillows and read with the same skill. Even the boy he'd earlier pegged "the class terror" read well.

Before he realized it, an hour had passed. Ricardo glanced up with a vague sense of guilt and his gaze met Angela's. She knew. He'd become involved with the students and had forgotten the purpose of his visit.

He swore silently. She'd tricked him by sending her top students to distract him. A quick survey of the classroom revealed total chaos. Two children were under their desks. Four were sitting at a table talking. Several others were walking around the classroom while another scribbled on the chalkboard. He groaned.

To top it off, Angela wasn't teaching. Come to think of it, she hadn't spoken to the class once since directing them earlier. She'd spent the whole morning sitting at the table in the corner, talking with one or two children at a time.

Ricardo swore to keep one eye on Miss Angela Stuart, no matter how fascinating the children were.

The next hour flew as rapidly as the first. It proved to be more difficult to maintain his surveillance of Angela than he'd thought. The students constantly demanded his attention. He heard more stories, spelled words and helped with mathematics until he felt exhausted.

Finally, she announced lunchtime. Relieved, he helped the children line up. Where had the morning gone? He'd only meant to spend an hour in Angela's class, but he found himself unwilling to leave.

"Did you enjoy your morning, Mr. de la Cruz?" She approached him after seeing the students out the door.

Ricardo frowned. "We need to talk."

"Yes, I'd like to know your reaction."

He saw the wariness creep into her eyes when she noticed his frown. "Can I take you to lunch?" he offered.

"I have playground duty today," she said as she glanced at her watch. "I won't be free until after the children go home."

Probably seeing her later was for the best. She'd want his reaction, and he needed to organize his thoughts. "I'll be back when your class lets out."

"Fine, Mr. de la Cruz."

"Ricardo," he corrected, inviting her to use his given name. He reached up, unable to resist brushing back the wayward strand of hair that had escaped the bun at the nape of her neck. Her fragrance teased his senses. Slowly he lowered his hand and backed away. *"Hasta luego."* He smiled and left.

FOR THE FIRST TIME since she'd begun teaching, Angela watched the clock. The afternoon seemed to drag. What had Ricardo de la Cruz mean by his remark, "We need to talk"? As her tension increased, she grew annoyed. He could have told her *something* before he left—like he was impressed with the class or that he hated it. Why did he leave her to spend the afternoon worrying?

Furthermore, she scolded herself, why *was* she worrying? She should be confident enough in herself to accept whatever opinion he held.

But she wasn't that confident. Not since Yuma. Was it going to happen again? Would she lose her teaching position? Flushing, Angela remembered the humiliation and pain. She couldn't go through that again—and wouldn't. *No.* She loved her present job and would fight to keep it.

Calmed by her resolution, Angela turned her attention back to her class, but the noise and activity couldn't keep her mind off Ricardo de la Cruz.

She'd been watching him at board meetings for several months now and had to admire his ability to act swiftly and efficiently. He wasn't afraid to explore new ways of tackling a problem. If she could persuade him to support her methods, he'd be a strong ally in the district.

It seemed ages, but the afternoon did come to a close. Angela bent down to hug her students as they said goodbye. Even though she was relieved to see them go, their affection gave her a momentary respite from her uneasiness.

"It's obvious they love their teacher." His deep voice came from outside the doorway.

Angela straightened. She had been so busy dismissing her students that she hadn't seen him standing there. She felt at a disadvantage, as if he'd witnessed a private part of herself.

"They always hug me goodbye," she explained.

"I remember wanting to do that when I was in first grade, but I was too terrified."

"I can't imagine you terrified of anything," she countered, and stepped back into the classroom, gesturing him to follow her.

"It wasn't the teacher I was afraid of," he told her as he entered the room, "but the other boys. I thought they'd beat me up."

Angela laughed, guessing full well that he was lying. Picturing Ricardo de la Cruz afraid even as a young boy proved difficult. Furthermore, she doubted that he'd ever cared what others thought of him, but she recognized his attempt to ease her tension and appreciated it.

Angela brought a chair over to her desk and offered it to him, and then she sat down. She hadn't been this nervous since her first year of teaching in the Arizona border town of Yuma. She recalled meeting Steve Daniels, the principal, and how awed she'd been by him at first. But then they'd become friends—more than friends. Thinking of the disaster of their relationship made her resolve never again to get involved with anyone who could have a detrimental effect on her teaching career.

"So, tell me, Mr. de la Cruz—" she smiled, determined not to let him detect her turmoil "—what did you think of my classroom and the whole-language program?"

"Ricardo, remember?" He smiled back, but Angela could sense a hesitancy. "It's obvious you care for your students and that they care for you. You have a way with them that makes them proud of themselves."

He paused, and Angela could almost hear the "But..." She took a deep breath. *Here it comes*, she thought, and she braced herself for defense.

"Your methods are unorthodox," he told her bluntly.

"Of course," she blurted. "That's been our main objective."

"But how can you teach with all that disorder?" he asked her.

"There was *no* disorder, Mr. de la Cruz." She watched him sigh at her purposeful use of his formal name. "Every student knew exactly what work he had to do and when it had to be completed."

"But is it possible for them to work with such noise and confusion?"

"There was little confusion, and the noise was productive." Angela stood and began to pace. She was gearing up for her lecture. "Did you listen to the conversations going on around you?"

"No," he admitted while he rose and followed her across the small open space between tables.

"Listen to them next time. You'll find their conversation enlightening." She was on a roll now. "They're usually discussing their classwork, thinking out loud or seeking help."

"First-graders," he scoffed, and ran his finger along his jaw. "I find that an overoptimistic view of their capabilities."

"Which is the attitude traditional education has maintained," she persisted, standing with hands on her hips. "We have this strange idea that a child can't learn one concept until he's mastered others. Recent studies are proving that's not true."

"You mean a child can read and write before he knows the alphabet?" His look of confidence spoke volumes. He thought he had her now, but she knew differently.

"Right." She surprised him by confirming his conjecture. She pointed to the students' work on the walls.

"It happens quite often. Actually it's been proven that most children can recognize words before they go to school."

"I have preschool nieces and nephews who are considered bright," he interrupted her, "and they don't read." He stared with concentration.

"Ask them to pick out their favorite cereal or where they want to eat lunch." Angela tried not to let his gaze unnerve her. "It's been proven that preschool children can read labels, signs and logos."

"They're just recognizing pictures."

"Part of the time that's true, but researchers have isolated the writing from the pictures and the preschoolers still recognize the words," she pointed out. "But consider this. The child is learning to associate symbols for something that has meaning to them. They do this in the same way they associate verbal symbols to situations. If their mother says the word *Pepsi*, they think soda pop. When the word *Pepsi* occurs in writing in the same context, they learn to read the word."

"Assuming you're right," he said, apparently not conceding, "it still doesn't justify chaos in the classroom."

"I presume you think a classroom should be all neat rows of desks with absolute silence prevailing?" she asked, while tapping her foot.

He wasn't going to get away without understanding the concept of whole language. She had to convince him that speaking and listening, reading and writing, are interrelated; and that acquiring and developing these skills occurs best in a noncompetitive environment where learning activities are set up to encourage children to practice using all four aspects of language.

"The quality classrooms I've observed since becoming a board member have been exactly that." He spoke with a measure of determination and walked toward her. "Also, the teacher is standing in front of the classroom, teaching her students."

"Most classrooms are still like that," she admitted.

It was this very aspect of the program that upset parents and observers the most. Her classroom didn't operate in the way they were used to, so they often had difficulty understanding what was happening. They were too busy focusing on what they thought was disruptive behavior to see that the children were actually performing at a level far higher than what was previously believed capable of first-grade students.

Part of the reason they didn't see it was because the students were so relaxed and happy. They shared knowledge through interaction, thus giving themselves a larger base of information and reference.

She had to explain how critical the issue was. "Have you read the report of the President's task force on education? We are a nation at risk, Mr. de la Cruz."

Angela paused for effect.

"Our traditional schools are not producing students who can think for themselves, or comprehend what they read. We have high dropout rates." She gestured in triumph. He couldn't argue with these facts. "And it's largely because we have classrooms of silence where the students aren't allowed to think. All day long they are directed to fill in blanks on meaningless sheets of paper in the form of workbooks and photocopies."

"You're talking about skills," he interjected. "Skills necessary to learn the basics."

"But skills taught in that manner have no meaning to the students. They rarely relate them to the real world." She sighed with dismay. It was obvious he agreed with the "back-to-the-basics" panacea for the ills of the educational system. It was still a popular movement among conservative school boards in the state. The problem was, the research she'd been involved in was proving those methods were the *cause* of some of the problems, not the *cure*. You couldn't teach reading through a hierarchy of skills, as if it were an assembly line.

Well, she'd just have to prove to him that the whole-language process she followed was educationally sound. Ricardo de la Cruz was intelligent and, judging from her observation of his actions on the board and on television, open to new ideas. He had a reputation for investigating all sides of an issue. It would be up to her to show him her side. Straightening her shoulders, she continued.

"Mr. de la Cruz, I have a proposition I'd like to make."

The challenge in her tone caught his attention. The faint lines radiating from the corners of his eyes creased as he focused on her.

"You come and observe my class for a whole week," she proposed. "And then you can tell me what effective education is."

"I can tell you now, Miss Stuart," he assured her. "I doubt you'll convince me that competent teaching involves children crawling around on the floor while you sit *visiting* with your students."

"You have no idea what those students on the floor were doing, nor obviously what *I* accomplished," she protested, feeling an odd mixture of indignation and disappointment. Surely the Ricardo de la Cruz she admired couldn't be this determined not to give her a chance. "As a reporter, you should know that first impressions seldom reveal the underlying facts. Investigate the evidence, Mr. de la Cruz, and you'll see what I'm talking about."

Amusement danced in his eyes and Angela took a step back. She'd challenged him on a matter of principle—and he was laughing?

"All right, Miss Stuart," he replied. "I concede your point. I'll come visit. Perhaps in that time I'll be able to listen to your *regular* students, not just the selected top."

So that's what he thought. Angela couldn't mask her smile.

"You *didn't* meet the top today, Mr. de la Cruz. They were at another school where they attend the gifted-students program twice a week."

The look of surprise on his face made the difficult day's ordeal worthwhile for Angela.

"I see," he stated, rocking back on his heels while assessing her carefully. "I'll have to clear my calendar and check with the station. It should only take a couple of days."

"Fine." Angela extended her arm to shake on the agreement. "Why don't you begin next Monday?"

"Monday it is." He took her hand.

She had won the first round.

"Nice to finally meet you, Mr. de la Cruz." She meant that, even though he'd been stubborn about her issue.

"Ricardo, remember." He winked, disarming her totally.

"Ricardo," she murmured, liking the way the Spanish name rolled across her tongue. She started to withdraw her hand, but he held on. Surprised, she glanced up and their gazes met. Alarmed, she stepped back.

He let go and turned toward the door. "Until Monday," he said. With a confidant wave, he strode out of the room.

2

ANGELA LET OUT A SIGH of relief. She'd wanted to meet Ricardo de la Cruz for months, but never dreamed it would be under these circumstances.

Still, she'd held her own. He loved dealing with issues, and now Angela had provided him with one.

Her mind churning with ideas, she set about making preparations for the next day's instruction. Without a doubt, she'd make her point clear. Ricardo de la Cruz would recognize the value of her teaching techniques—or he wasn't the man she thought him to be.

Wrapped up in her plans, Angela didn't hear the door open. Startled, she jumped when Maria spoke.

"So, how did it go?"

"Don't come up on me like that," Angela chided her friend.

"Was it that bad, or is it your usual end-of-the-day touchiness?"

"You know I'm always grumpy after teaching." Feeling drained, Angela hung up the last drawing on the wall and stepped back with a sigh of relief. She looked at Maria's energetic smile and groaned. "How do you always stay so chipper? Don't you ever get tired?"

"I'm just finally waking up about now. You know I'm a night person." Maria chuckled, settling on the corner of the table. "So, tell me. How did it go?"

Angela made a face.

"Not good, huh? Did your class blow it?"

"They were great, as always," Angela said, defending her students. "It was him." She threw up her hands in disgust. "He came in with his mind made up and missed all the important things."

"I find that hard to believe," Maria commented. "He's a thorough investigator."

"So I thought." Angela began sorting papers. "But you know how slow people are to change their views on education. Look how long it took us to get some of the teachers to understand our methods. I'd just hoped that de la Cruz would be different."

"Maybe he was too busy watching *you* instead of seeing what was going on," Maria suggested.

"What are you talking about?"

"I've seen the way he looks at you during the board meetings. Don't tell me he's not interested in more than your teaching." Maria crossed her arms and smiled.

"Ridiculous," Angela scoffed.

"Could be." Maria shrugged. "But I don't think so."

"I hope you're wrong, Maria. You *have* to be wrong."

"What's the matter with male interest? It couldn't hurt your cause."

"No way. I'm never getting involved with anyone even remotely connected with my work again." Angela began vigorously erasing the chalkboard.

"You mean because of what happened in Yuma?"

Angela nodded.

"That was six years ago, and a different situation."

Angela didn't want to be reminded of the past. She needed all of her energy for the present. "You're right. It was a long time ago and I'm not repeating past mistakes."

"Okay, okay." Maria threw up her hands and laughed. "Let's hear about what happened. Just the straight facts—no emotional stuff."

Angela shook her head and laughed. Maria could be counted on to see the bright side of any situation. Thinking it might help, Angela related the events of the day while she measured out new paint for the easels.

"You're kidding." Maria whistled. "He's going to be here a whole week?"

"If I survive," Angela confirmed ruefully.

"If you get tired of him, he can come to my room. I'd love to take care of that hunk."

"Don't tease," Angela warned. "I just might send him over, and then what would you do?"

"I'd manage to keep him busy. *I* don't have any hang-ups about involvement with school personnel," Maria said.

"Don't you have work to do?"

"Yes, but this is more fun."

"Will this day never end?" Angela rolled her eyes upward and sighed. "These journals the children wrote need to be answered." She gestured to the pile of notebooks on the table, hoping Maria would take the hint and leave her in peace.

"Okay, okay," Maria capitulated. "I'll go." She paused in the doorway. "Do you want a ride home?"

"No, thanks. It's out of your way."

"I don't mind."

"Really, I'd rather take the bus." Angela appreciated her friend's offer, but all she wanted now was to be left alone.

"You just want to finish the book you're reading."

"Right." Angela waved off her friend. Maria often teased her about taking the bus when she had a car she could drive to school. But Angela enjoyed the half hour it took to arrive at her east-side apartment.

She glanced up at the clock. An hour to go and she still had so much to do. At least tomorrow was Friday. The weekend was almost here and she'd be at her folks' on Sunday. That would cheer her up.

FRIDAY AFTERNOON, Ricardo sat in front of the school waiting for Angela. She was late. School had let out an hour ago. He drummed his fingers on the leather casing of the steering wheel. Wouldn't the *cholos*, the gang he'd grown up with, laugh at him if they saw him now— hanging around a *school*. Ricardo de la Cruz—a dropout from junior high.

Ricardo shook his head at the memories. His parents had been disappointed when he'd decided to quit school—especially his father. But at thirteen, he thought he knew it all. What was the use of going to school when his olive skin and heavy accent barred him from achieving the American Dream. But he'd been wrong. Dead wrong. His attitude had really just been a cop-out to avoid the work and effort it took for him to "make it."

The engine of the black Ferrari convertible roared when Ricardo pressed the accelerator. He loved his car and, true, at times admittedly acted like a teenager with it. But he'd never had a decent car as a kid. Finally, when he was in his twenties and making money, he'd put all his earnings into the older-model sports car, figuring he deserved his fun. He gunned the sleek machine again. Was it because he was showing off or because his muscles had tensed at the sight of Angela as she came through the school gate? *Both,* he admitted.

She walked toward him and smiled when she spotted him.

"Quite a car. It suits you." Her voice sounded like velvet. Just like he remembered.

"I'm not sure I want to know what you mean." He watched her slender fingers smooth over the shiny finish of the passenger door and suddenly imagined them tracing across his skin. "You don't mean vintage, I hope."

"Bold. Daring." A hint of teasing twinkled in her eyes. "Showy, too."

"You're not implying that I'm a show-off, are you?"

She grinned.

Ricardo felt an urge to pull her down into his lap. Instead, he opened his door.

"I didn't expect to see you until Monday," she commented, her expression serious now.

"After we talked yesterday I went to the station," he told her as he stepped out of the car. "It took some maneuvering, but we're set for Monday."

"Great."

"Yes and no." He walked around the front of the car. "They released me for Monday, but not the whole week." He lifted his hand against her expression of protest. "We compromised. I can come every Monday for a month—providing the station doesn't have any emergencies to cover."

"That's fair."

"How about going for a drink and discussing the details?" he offered. He began to take the heavy bag from her hand, never expecting her to refuse.

"I can't." She tugged on the handle but Ricardo didn't let go. "I have to make a visit to a student at home."

"It's Friday." He stared in surprise and then gestured to the empty parking lot. "And past time to go home."

There was no way he'd let her get away. He'd been waiting for half an hour. She looked around and appeared annoyed that the hour had grown so late. Her grip on the bag loosened and Ricardo quickly set it in the back.

"Hop in," he told her. He could see it was time someone reminded her that there was a time for work and a time for play. "Surely you won't be working any more today."

"I'll go," she conceded. "But first I need to drop these off at Mariana's house. She lives just around the corner."

"Stubborn," he accused her.

"She's been sick and I promised I'd take her some homework."

He settled her on the cream leather seat and closed the door. She looked terrific sitting in his car, her blond hair contrasting with the shiny black exterior. It only took minutes to drive to Mariana's. The house was dilapidated, but that wasn't where she headed when he stopped at the curb. A shed in even worse shape than the house stood out back in the dirt yard.

Several bare-chested men lounged under a tree with cans of beer in their hands and cigarettes dangling from their fingers. They stopped talking and every pair of eyes focused on Angela's approach.

Alarmed, Ricardo slid out of the car and hurried to catch up with her. He soon discovered his concern to be unnecessary. Every man stood at attention and greeted her with respect when she passed them by. They assessed Ricardo until he felt compelled to place a familiar hand at her elbow. Then he smiled and nodded a curt hello as he guided her inside the shack.

Ricardo watched with growing interest as Angela made herself at home in the crowded but clean interior. She casually sat on the edge of the bed that nearly filled the single room.

"*¡Hola!* Hi. Are you feeling better?" she asked in her accented Spanish to the frail girl tucked under the covers.

Ricardo leaned against the door frame and silently waited. "Homework," she'd said. He laughed to himself. A pack of papers *did* appear from her bag, but so did a Barbie doll, a storybook and a bag of oranges she claimed were off her tree. He noticed the obvious affection Mariana and her family had for Angela.

What a shame that her teaching methods couldn't be commended! She truly cared about her students and had won their respect. Teachers who showed genuine enthusiasm for students from the inner-city barrios were rare. Her warmth and caring certainly contrasted with the teachers he had had. Most had been cold and strict, rigid and irritated with his curiosity and outspokenness.

Even the school buildings themselves were worlds apart. His school had been an ancient brick structure covered with graffiti and sporting broken windows. Schools like the one where Angela taught were brandnew, with landscaped gardens. Constructed in the Southwestern desert style, the low buildings wrapped around an inner courtyard. Yet they hadn't always been like that. Only five years ago, they'd been condemned by the fire marshal. Getting the community to vote for the building of new schools was one of the accomplishments he was most proud of.

The whimpers of a baby interrupted his thoughts. He hadn't noticed the infant sleeping on the other side of Mariana.

"¡Mira!" Angela exclaimed, and leaning over, picked up the little boy. His tiny arms and legs stretched out with delight at being held. Angela pressed him close against her breast.

"Isn't he precious?" Angela smiled and the mother beamed with pride.

The baby's curly black hair stood out against the yellow dress Angela wore. He pressed his tiny face and hands into her curves. The sight touched a tender chord within Ricardo. He wasn't sure he felt comfortable about it.

The woman was doing it to him again. In spite of all the professional reservations he had about her, personally, she intrigued him.

When they returned to the car, she said, "I could use that drink you offered now."

"You've got it," he assured her.

"Do you make a lot of home visits?" he asked.

"When I need to."

"Most teachers don't bother."

"Most teachers don't have the time," she countered.

"But you find time," he pointed out.

"I don't have a husband and children at home waiting for their supper, either," she told him. Was there a wistful tone in her voice?

Ricardo changed the subject. "Aren't you frightened, coming into this neighborhood?"

She glanced over at him and then laughed. The sound of it wafted through him like a pleasant melody.

"I'm safer in this neighborhood than in my own," she said.

"How's that?"

"Everyone knows me, and besides, most of these people are from Mexico. Teachers are held in high esteem there."

"Is that why you teach in the barrio?" He sensed that her reasons for being here went deeper than the higher salary the inner-city district offered.

"Partly." She cast him an accusing stare. "Teachers don't always get much respect in this country, especially after news specials like the one your station did."

Dangerous ground. Recalling the special aired last month, he grimaced. In the program's analysis of Arizona's education system, teachers hadn't fared well. "They only showed the facts."

"As they saw them," she added pointedly.

"Let's be fair. I'm spending several days in your class." He shrugged and down-shifted for the red light. He wasn't going to apologize, so he attempted to change the subject. "You said 'partly.' What are your other reasons for teaching here?"

Her brow burrowed in concentration, making him wonder why she hesitated. Finally she spoke: "It's complicated and involved."

"I'm interested," he prodded.

"The main reason I'm at this particular district is because of Dr. Wheeler. She and the others wanted to prove their theory that present-day educators are using the wrong methods and—"

Ricardo interrupted. "Why Valley of the Sun district to prove that?"

"Five years ago, our school had the lowest test scores in the state. You should know that."

He was surprised at how bitter he still felt about it. He glanced at her. "And now?"

"They're up quite a bit."

Why hadn't he heard *that* before? He'd do some more checking—soon.

He knew she was waiting for a reaction. "I'm impressed." He paused for a moment. "It doesn't seem to bother you to work with these kids."

The statement was loaded and he knew she knew it.

"Should it bother me?"

Ricardo shrugged. "Being in the barrio upsets some." Several unpleasant experiences of his youth flashed in his mind.

"If we're speaking about prejudice—" her glance reflected earnest conviction "—then you must know that the only way to fight it is to build the students' confidence and sense of self-worth."

He couldn't fault her there. Her students exhibited a pride in themselves.

"You're confident and self-assured," she observed. "How did you develop such strength of character?"

Her question took him by surprise. His father's love and understanding had instilled in him an unwavering sense of self-worth—pride that healed the wounds of youthful hurt and anger. Ricardo wasn't ready to talk about his past. He didn't want her penetrating his reserve and besides, it was too painful to recall the memories of his deceased father. "It's a long story. One you wouldn't want to hear."

"Sorry." She didn't press him but began to rub her aching temples. "It's nice of you to give me a ride. I'm exhausted."

"I know just the place for you." He turned off Central Avenue. It was time to ease up and relax.

3

ANGELA SCOWLED at herself in the mirror of the ladies' room, then blotted her lipstick and ran a comb through her hair. What was she doing here—at a restaurant— with a man who had the power to threaten her job? It was against all her rules.

There was nothing she could do about it now. *So stop worrying*, she ordered herself. Nothing would happen. After all, having dinner with him didn't mean a thing. Did it?

Walking back to the table, Angela carefully observed Ricardo. His eyes were alert, obviously taking in every detail around him. His hair, windblown from the convertible, looked as if someone had run lazy fingers through it. He'd removed his jacket. His blue shirt stretched across his shoulders, outlining a well-muscled back.

"How do you do it?" he asked after he seated her across from him.

"What's that?" She looked up.

"I've seen you at school looking cool and efficient. You seemed maternal and sweet with a baby in your arms." He gestured to their surroundings. "And now you sit across from me, here, looking sophisticated. All of these different faces in the space of one hour. It boggles the mind."

Flattered, she lifted a glass of the wine they'd been served.

"Here's to the many facets of life," she toasted.

"Here's to you," he shot back.

Pleased by the compliments, she smiled before sipping the chilled wine. The muted glow of the candlelight and the quiet dinner music soothed her.

"Angela, when I come in next Monday—" he spoke in serious tones now "—I want to bring my cameraman and videotape your class."

Suddenly tense and alert, she asked sharply. "Why?"

"For one thing, we can observe your techniques, and you can explain to me the theory behind your methods."

"You need your television crew to do that?"

"It wouldn't be for the station. My cameraman owes me a favor. I put in a lot of extra research hours for a photojournal piece that won Ken an award so he owes me some time. We can come over on our days off and tape."

"And will this be used for another television special?" She could picture it now. Broadcast headlines. "I don't think so."

"Look, you've got a lot going for you." He leaned close. "You relate to your students. That's more than most teachers do."

"How generous." Angela bit her tongue to prevent herself from telling him where he could go with his compliments.

"Stop taking this negatively," he advised, reaching across the table to cover her fingers.

Angela snatched her hand away. His eyes narrowed.

"I only want to help you."

"And you think by videotaping my classroom you can give me advice on how to teach?"

"We can work on it together."

"You are an expert on education?" she asked him with a touch of sarcasm.

"No, but when we look . . ."

"Mr. de la Cruz." She sat up straighter and stared him in the eye. "I have spent the past five years developing the whole-language approach that I'm practicing now."

He shook his head. "All the studying in the world doesn't show up in practice. I've seen—"

"I said developing, Mr. de la Cruz," she interrupted him. "I have been working with professors from Arizona State University who are experts in the field—Ph.D.s with national recognition for their theories on whole-language and holistic teaching. Whole-language means learning all aspects of language at one time—learning to talk and write and read about a subject that's relevant and interesting to the children at a specific time. We try to show how reading and writing are tools to help them learn about the world—and also that they're tools for expressing their feelings about what is important to them."

"That's just it. Theories don't always work in the real world."

"Which is exactly my part in their research," Angela continued, undaunted by his biased response. "I'm putting whole-language theories about how children learn—especially how they become literate—into practice. And they're working."

"I didn't see learning. I saw a noisy, chaotic classroom. There were students scribbling on paper, they were talking all the time, and they rarely sat down."

His earnest concern stilled some of the defensiveness rising inside her. He really cared, and instead of antagonizing him, she should use that caring to her advantage.

"You mentioned you have nieces and nephews." She forced herself to sound calm.

He nodded, obviously puzzled by her change of subject.

"Remember when they learned to talk? Did their parents sit them down and force them to be quiet while they drilled them on the sounds? Did they flash cards in their faces to teach them the words?"

"Don't be ridiculous, we're talking about—"

"The way children learn," she interrupted, ignoring the annoyance crossing his features.

"Did someone make them practice the saying *m, m, m,* so they'd be able to say Mama?" Angela leaned forward, excited now about the point she was about to make. "Of course not. We talk to a baby as if he or she already understands. The baby relates what he hears to the world around him.

"Children need that same interaction to learn to read. They need to attach the written word to what's going on in their world. That's why you need a classroom that allows risk-taking and freedom to explore."

"That makes sense," he conceded. "But I don't understand how it works. Don't you see how the videos will be a tool to help explain the process?"

"I don't think so. We've worked too long and hard to have our efforts made into a sham."

"Now, just a minute. I have no intention of turning this into a sham. Did you consider that the tapes may prove me wrong?"

Anger glinted in his dark eyes and Angela matched it with her own. She vowed to show this arrogant know-it-all—

"Your wine, sir," the waiter interrupted. Frustrated, she watched the waiter pour more wine and leave.

Suddenly Ricardo reached across the table to place a rough finger against her mouth. In spite of her anger, she tingled with pleasure.

"Enough. I want us to enjoy our meal together."

Before Angela could protest, he lightly caressed her lips.

All thoughts of their discussion vanished.

Angela couldn't see the other diners. The room receded until there were only the two of them.

He bent his head and shook it. "I shouldn't have done—" He started to apologize but Angela placed her fingers against his.

She wanted to tell him not to regret such a moment, but words failed her.

Seconds passed before she began to lower her hand. Ricardo captured her wrist and started to bring her fingers to his lips when the aroma of chicken and herbs suddenly brought them back to reality. Angela looked past Ricardo's shoulder to see the waiter holding two steaming plates.

Ricardo followed her gaze and straightened, releasing her hand. A reckless grin lit up his features.

"Looks good," she commented while she eyed the plate of chicken-and-cashew embedded in the hollowed-out pineapple.

"I'm glad you're hungry," he told her after thanking the waiter. "My last meal was breakfast."

"Don't tell me you work through lunches, too," she teased.

"When necessary. But enough about work. Tell me, what are some of your interests outside of school?"

"I like to read," she told him as she tasted the lanai.

"What? No television?" He sent her a mock scowl.

"Only the news," she admitted, but didn't dare mention she watched Channel Four just to see him. Often she had no idea what else had been reported.

"That's a relief. I like old movies, myself. Hardly ever read." He took a bite and after swallowing, traced his tongue across his lips.

The action attracted her full attention. Angela sat, fork poised midway to her plate and licked her own lips. She couldn't even remember what they'd been discussing.

"What about music? I'm into hard rock."

It took a moment, but his question finally registered. Angela quickly finished the bite and hoped he hadn't noticed her distraction. But the glints of humor in his eyes denied that wish. "New Age music, soft and harmonious."

He groaned.

"You must like fast dancing?"

He nodded and said, "And I bet you're into slow and easy."

She smiled.

"Hmm. Seems like we have nothing in common."

"I bet I can guess one thing." She eyed his lean physique. "I jog every morning."

"Jog?" He set down his fork with a shudder. "If it's more than half a block, I drive."

Angela leaned back in her chair and let her delight in their light banter flow through her. They did have opposite interests, but maybe that was good.

"I suppose I'd drive everywhere, too, if I had a Ferrari."

"I didn't always have a car like that." His expression turned serious.

Interested, Angela leaned forward. "Tell me about your childhood. Did you grow up here?"

"East L.A." He went on to provide a few highlights, but the longer he talked the more serious he became.

Angela's heart went out to Ricardo as he talked. She wondered what had made him so confident and sure of who he was.

"My father died when I was sixteen," Ricardo said as he finished his last bite. "He was the kindest man I've ever known and I miss him still. But his death brought me around."

"You're so different from the angry, bitter teenager you've been describing."

"I had reason to be angry. My father's death was unnecessary. He worked in a garment factory. Everyone knew it was one of the unsafe, outdated pieces of machinery that had killed him. But the facts were covered up with the help of bribes to the police and lies to the press."

In his eyes, Angela glimpsed the turmoil he'd suffered. Yet she still couldn't connect the boy with the man.

"It was my mother who finally brought me around to direct all that negative energy into a positive outlet." He finished his wine and gripped the stem of the glass. "She told me nothing could be done and I took that as a personal challenge. I vowed I'd go to school and place myself in a position of power where I could act upon corruption and change social conditions."

Now she understood the drive and energy he exuded. It also gave her hope. Surely his basic integrity and honesty would make him see that her methods worked and he would judge her fairly.

The waiter came to pour wine again and asked if they wanted dessert. Angela refused. So did Ricardo. But the interruption broke the intensity of their conversation. Ricardo sent her a rueful smile.

"I suppose I've gotten a little heavy-duty here. I didn't mean to spill my guts, especially since we hardly know each other."

"Don't be sorry. It gives me hope to hear your story."

"Hope?"

"Any man who can admit his mistakes and grow from them won't find it difficult to admit being wrong about my teaching."

Ricardo stared for a moment and then threw back his head and laughed. So did Angela, but more so from relief. She hadn't been all that sure of her bold supposition.

The waiter brought them steaming cups of coffee after their plates had been cleared. Ricardo leaned forward.

"That brings us back to school, doesn't it? Are you going to let me video your class?"

Angela eyed him with wariness, not wanting to return to the subject of school.

"My major concern is my students." She evaded his question. "I don't want my classroom disrupted with camera and crew."

Braced for a protest, his next move took her by surprise. He didn't argue, but leaned back in his chair and grinned. Angela straightened in her seat. Now she knew that he wasn't to be trusted. She had seen this tactic before during board meetings: Relax your opponent and then thrust swift and deep.

"You do have a fine bunch of students in your class," he complimented her.

"They are," she agreed, watching him closely.

"I admire teachers who dedicate themselves to their students," he continued. "You're one of those."

"I try to be," she responded, wondering what he was getting at.

"I bet you do everything in your power to improve their lot. Even make sacrifices."

"It's part of the job." If he thought she would sit and pat herself on the back, he was wrong. She made sacrifices, but they were her choice and not something done to attract extra attention.

"I would even go so far as to bet that you'd risk your job to fight battles for them."

"Is that what I'm going to have to do?" In spite of her bravado, fear began to form. Angela loved teaching. Losing her position would be a painful price to pay. Having to leave Yuma had cost her many bitter tears.

"No, I didn't mean that." He leaned forward to reassure her, appearing to regret his choice of words. "I find it hard to believe that a teacher with such devotion wouldn't agree to a simple request to videotape her teaching."

Back to the taping again. Fear of losing her job vanished. Thoughts of admiration and respect fizzled. He'd pretended to be interested in her as a woman and then *bam!* Attack. Annoyed and hurt, Angela stood.

"I will not be manipulated, Mr. de la Cruz." Oh, he was good. He almost had her there. Soften her up with good food and stories of his childhood, and then he had the nerve to play on her sense of dedication. *What a snake!*

Rummaging through her purse, she searched out her money. Thank goodness she had cashed a check last night. She found the crumpled bills and set them on the table. "Good night!"

"Angela," he protested. His muttered oaths reached her ears in spite of the widening distance between them.

Once outside, she stopped. The steam that had propelled her to this point suddenly evaporated. Where could she go with no car?

"It will take an hour for a cab to get out this far," he said from behind her.

Phoenix, after dark, was impossible to get around in. Her options were to wait the hour or swallow her pride and go with Ricardo. It had been a long, trying day.

"Looks like I need a ride." And she'd slug him if he became smug about it.

Gripping her arm easily, just above her elbow, he guided her toward the Ferrari. "I'll have you home in no time."

Seated and comfortable in the sporty car, Angela stole a glance at Ricardo. At the same time, he peered across the small space at her. His contrite expression made her laugh. And the responding look of surprise on his face made her laugh all the harder.

"Care to share the joke?" She couldn't tell if he was smiling or frowning.

"You have to admit," she managed between chuckles, "it ruined my grand exit to be stranded without a car."

"You made your point." He reached over and patted her hand. "Does that make you feel any better?"

"No." She leaned her head back against the headrest and closed her eyes. The warmth from his hand seeped into hers.

Suddenly it didn't seem so important to resist the videotaping. If she were smart, she could use it to her advantage. Analyzing each aspect of the students' classroom behavior would prove to him that her methods had merit.

"I'll agree to the video," she told him. "On one condition."

"Which is?"

"We go over the tapes together. You promise to spend time with me to analyze what's seen."

"That won't be a problem."

The rest of the ride to her apartment complex passed in silence. When he pulled around the circular driveway for guests, she gathered her purse and bag.

"You can just drop me off," she told him before he cut the engine. "It's early still."

"Okay." He relented after studying her determined expression. "We'll be at your classroom at eight o'clock to set up our equipment."

"Will you need anything special?"

"No. Everything's portable. Teach your regular lessons, like you do every day."

"That's the main idea," she said with a hint of sarcasm.

He laughed while he stepped out of the car to come around and open her door. She ignored him, unable to muster indignation now.

"I enjoyed the dinner," she offered with sincerity as she stepped out of the low-slung car. There'd been moments of pleasure during their meal—moments when she was totally aware of her companion. As she was now.

Her shoulder brushed against the lapel of his linen sports jacket when she stood.

"Until Monday, then," she murmured. An absurd desire to invite him up to her apartment nudged at her

common sense. He hesitated as if the same thought had
crossed his mind. With a catch in her throat, Angela
spun around and hurried toward the inner courtyard
of the complex. She listened, and was half disappointed when no footsteps followed.

RICARDO PURPOSEFULLY strode through the courtyard
filled with Saturday-afternoon sunbathers. Intent on
his goal—Angela's apartment, number twenty-four, he
wound his way through the shrubbery. Impatient. Annoyed. After all he'd gone through to get Angela to
agree to his taping her class, and now this. His editor
couldn't have picked a worse time to send him out on
assignment.

Her apartment faced the inner courtyard on the
ground level. He peered in the large window as he
passed but saw no sign of her. As he knocked on the
door, he felt a thread of anticipation weave through the
frustration.

"Madre mío," he swore as he searched his pockets for
the pad and pencil he always carried. A note. It was a
hell of a way to tell her. The right words wouldn't come.
He stood, pencil poised, his mind a blank.

"You looking for Miss Stuart?" a child's voice came
from the vicinity of his knee.

Ricardo peered past his notebook at the dark-eyed
girl looking up at him. One of Angela's students. He
recognized the toothless smile.

"Is she here?" He bent down to balance on his heels.

"She's by the pool." The girl hugged a bright beach
ball while she rocked on her toes.

"Aren't you from her class?"

"Sí." The child giggled. "Today is my turn to come
to her house."

"She brings all of you?" He raised his brows in disbelief.

"Only if we're good. Fernie never gets to come."

Ricardo struggled not to grin.

"Do you want me to get Miss Stuart?"

"No." He straightened his long legs. "I'll follow you."

In a flash the girl darted toward the pool. Ricardo shook his head. Damn the woman. Leave it to her to do something else to make his job more difficult. Imagine her bringing her students home—on her time off.

Yet he had to admit that she could make a person feel special. When he had sat across from her at dinner last night there hadn't been any of the nervous conversation that usually occurred between strangers. He had felt so comfortable and relaxed that he'd revealed things he rarely spoke of. She had a quality about her that made a person feel at ease, as if her world centered around him—even if it was only for that moment. He'd have to watch it, or he'd forget his purpose every time he was around her.

Cursing, he wound back through the shrubs. Reaching the patio, he searched the bronzed bodies splayed out on the lounge chairs. Too many men. He started wondering about Angela's social life.

A shimmer of turquoise caught his eye. Her blond hair hung over the back of the chaise lounge and her sleek curves were accented by suntan oil. The sight made his heart skip a beat. *¡Caramba!* She was beautiful. All thoughts of her being a teacher fled from his head. It was there again—the knowledge that he was man and she was woman. It was all that mattered now.

Suddenly she turned her head. The crowd around him ceased to exist. She was the only one there.

"Ricardo. Did you come to see me?" Surprise was evident in her expression, but he also detected a glimmer of pleasure.

"None other." He swaggered, full of confidence and expectancy. The purpose of his visit was the furthest thing from his mind. He sat down on the edge of her lounge and stretched over her to brace his weight on the far side. His body blocked the sun and cast a shadow across her. A look of concern replaced her smile, but Ricardo was certain he could conquer her doubts with his charm.

"What do you need?" she asked in a husky murmur.

You, he wanted to say. The heat from her sun-warmed skin reflected to his. The scent of suntan lotion carried her perfume with it. It would be so easy to bend over and kiss her. Their surroundings faded from his mind.

"Does there have to be a reason?"

"I would think so," she said with a puzzled glance.

Ricardo moved closer. Her tongue traced her lips and her breath caught in a short gasp. Ricardo could taste her already.

"Miss Stuart—" a high-pitched voice shattered the mood—"can I go in the water now?"

Ricardo straightened and smiled, his guilt making it a bit lopsided.

"In a minute, Lisa," she told her. "When I'm done talking to Mr. de la Cruz. Okay?"

Lisa spun around and trotted back to the children she had been playing with.

"I'm not used to having my moves on a lady interrupted by innocent bystanders," he informed her ruefully.

"Is that why you're here?"

"It wasn't my original intent, but it seemed like the right thing at the moment."

Angela placed her hand on his arm and shoved it aside, forcing him to sit up straight. Her long legs slipped off the lounge, bringing her close beside him.

"Why are you here?" She stood, putting herself at a safe distance from him.

Ricardo rose and followed her. She sat in a deck chair and with a gesture of her hand offered the empty one across from the small end table. *Smart move*, he acknowledged.

He sat down and answered, "Bad news, I'm afraid."

"Do I want to hear it?"

"I've been called out of town on an assignment." He saw her shoulders sag with relief and realized she had thought the bad news concerned her job. He wanted to reassure her, but he turned away and stared at his fingers clenched in a fist. "There's been an outbreak of violence at Copperville. The miners are on strike again. Since it's a couple hundred miles south of here I doubt I'll be back in time to come in as planned, on Monday."

"You won't be in danger, will you?"

Her concern touched him.

"I won't do anything foolish." He gave her the only promise he could. They sent him on this kind of assignment often. He was told it was because he was fearless and perhaps reckless, too. But he always came up with a dynamite story.

"When will you be back?" she asked.

"Depends. I'll get in touch when I do." He turned to face her and willed her to see his sincerity. "We're going to video your class. I promise."

With that, he stood and paused, wanting to succumb to the temptation that had tortured him since his arrival. He could almost feel the brush of his lips across her parted mouth. The imagined sweet taste of her sent shivers through him. And he wanted more—much more. Reluctantly he left the courtyard. He had to leave now or not at all.

"WHAT'RE YOU SO UPSET about?" Maria startled Angela with her question.

Angela glanced over at her friend who sat behind the wheel of her Mustang convertible as they drove east on McDowell Avenue. She'd offered to take Angela home, and today Angela had let her. Tired and preoccupied by thoughts of Ricardo, she'd been silent most of the way across town.

When Angela didn't answer, Maria went on, "It won't do any good to pretend you don't know what I'm talking about. Out with it."

Angela knew Maria wouldn't leave her alone until she was satisfied with the truth, so she told her about Ricardo's visit, trying not to reveal her feelings for the reporter. Nonetheless, Maria zeroed right in on the source of the problem.

"You're attracted to him," she stated. "So, what's wrong with that?"

"Everything," Angela groaned. "I refuse to be interested in any man connected with my job."

"Why so stubborn on that point?" Maria stopped at a red light and glared at her friend. "Mike Garrett has been after you for months and you won't give him the time of day."

"That's not true." Angela stiffened. It had required skill and tact to fend off Mike's interest without hurting his feelings. "Since Steve, I refuse to date men I work with."

"Steve?" Maria's ebony eyebrows rose.

A sinking feeling settled over Angela. She knew she should explain who Steve was and what had happened in Yuma. When she spoke, there was a bitterness in her voice. "As you know, my first teaching job ended up a disaster. I fell in love with my principal."

"And he fired you for that?"

Steve had bowled her over. She probably would have married him in her innocent naiveté if one of her colleagues hadn't been so jealous.

"One of the teachers accused me of sleeping with him to get special privileges." Angela shuddered, remembering the pain of that awful time.

"That's ridiculous! Anyone who knows you, wouldn't believe that."

"But it was true."

"What?" Maria said with shock.

To this day, the confrontation with Steve remained vividly clear in her memory. Disgust and shame had swamped her then . . . and did now.

"I wasn't aware of it, but he did give me preferential treatment because of our relationship." She had been so naive not to notice she had the newest equipment, the best classroom.

"So what did you do?" Maria slowed down as they approached Angela's apartment.

"I left as soon as the year was over."

"It should have been him that left," Maria growled in defense of her friend.

"It was hard to come home with such a botched career and love life," Angela admitted. Thank goodness her family had provided the support she needed to get her back on her feet.

"So, you see why I can't allow myself to be interested in Ricardo."

"Well, it doesn't matter, anyway," Maria assured her. "I heard Cathy and Lupe talking in the lounge."

"What are those two up to now?" Angela never paid much attention to the worst gossips on the staff. The two teachers constantly found fault with their students, teachers and the school in general.

"Plenty, I would guess." Maria didn't hide the annoyance she felt. "They were telling all the other teachers that they had talked to Ricardo de la Cruz."

"Oh? What did he tell them?"

"They said he told them he would have you fired."

4

"WHAT?" ANGELA BRACED HER hand on the dashboard. "They're making it up."

The two women didn't like Angela and made no effort to disguise it. Angela wouldn't put it past them to come up with some lie just to upset her.

"I thought so, too." Maria shrugged. "So I asked them when and where. They said they were passing by the station where he works and saw him. They had a chance to talk before he left for Copperville."

Angela's heart sank. That sounded plausible.

"They even described his clothes—cotton slacks and a safari shirt," Maria continued.

Angela's hopes faded. He had worn a safari shirt the day he had stopped by the pool. She remembered, because she had wanted to toy with the buttons located at strategic places on his body.

Fool! she admonished herself. Manipulated by his charm, she had trusted him. Well, her guard was up now. Forewarned, she would be prepared. If he didn't acknowledge the value of her teaching after what she planned to put him through, he could only be classified as closed-minded. Ricardo de la Cruz was not ignorant. He would see for himself that he was wrong. And she would gloat over her success.

"So what're you going to do?" Maria asked.

"Prepare the big guns," Angela declared, sounding more confident than she felt. "I've got it," she sud-

denly announced, shifting in the bucket seat to face
Maria. "Can you take my class the afternoon of Ricardo's last visit?"

"Sure," Maria agreed.

"It doesn't matter—one afternoon off won't hurt."
Angela paced again. "It'll be for their good in the long
run."

"What're you going to do? What can I do to help?"

Angela shook her head in wonder at her friend's
continual support. Changing to a new program, no
matter how good it was, created stress. Oftentimes
when Angela had been frustrated or discouraged, Maria would pop into the room with encouraging words.

Maria's backing had been especially helpful whenever Cathy or Lupe were on the prowl and looking for
any chance to knock the program. At first Angela
thought the problem with the two teachers stemmed
from the fact that Lupe had been forced to teach a different grade level to make room for Angela's whole-
language class. She couldn't blame her for being annoyed. But it soon became obvious that there was more
to it than that.

Lupe and Cathy simply didn't like the program and
made every effort to criticize and question all aspects
of it. Often the attacks became personal and Maria in-
evitably stepped in to stand up for her. Still, Angela felt
guilty involving her friend this time. But then again, she
knew Maria would insist.

"He promised me a session to analyze the tapes. I'll
call the professors and get them to come, too." Angela
felt better now that she had set her course. "With all of
us there, he won't be able to refute what he sees."

"Why would that make any difference? You can explain better than the professors. They get all caught up in educational jargon."

"True, but that's not the point," Angela explained. "I'll have witnesses."

"Why do you need witnesses?" Maria frowned.

"The videos." Angela waved her hand with impatience. "If he edits them to discredit me, I'll have proof."

Angela saw the confusion on Maria's face. With a sigh, she stopped talking for a minute and took a deep breath to gather her thoughts.

"He could take out all of the meaningful conversation among the kids and just show them running around," Angela elaborated. "You know what my room looks like to a stranger."

Maria's eyes widened with concern. "He wouldn't do that, would he?"

"Remember two years ago when that reporter came to our school for the article on bilingual education? They cut our conversation to make it sound like we were against bilingual classrooms."

"Ricardo de la Cruz has too much integrity."

"What am I to think?" Disappointment mingled with anger. "Last week I would've agreed with you, but now—after Cathy and Lupe's remark—who knows?"

"Cathy and Lupe can't be trusted. I wouldn't take seriously a word they say," Maria advised.

"I'm not taking any chances. I can't afford to."

"I'll help all I can," Maria promised as she pulled up in front of Angela's apartment complex. "Just tell me what I need to do."

"Thanks, I will. I'll call the university this evening." Angela opened the car door and grabbed her belongings. "See you tomorrow."

Angela strode to her apartment, her mind racing a mile a minute. But it wasn't plans for her conversation with the professors that had her deep in thought.

Ricardo de la Cruz. How was she going to be able to keep an emotional distance from him when he was in her classroom?

Later that evening she asked herself the same question, as she tried to relax in her living room.

In spite of her attempts to ignore Ricardo, she had Channel Four tuned in for the news report. It was important to keep informed, she rationalized, but there were five other channels to choose from. *So change it!* she ordered herself.

Just when she reached over to grab the remote control, Ricardo's face appeared on the screen. Her hand froze in midair. Angela focused on the rugged features that had her in such turmoil. Exhaustion hollowed his cheeks and tension had deepened the tiny lines around his eyes. Concerned, Angela listened to the newscast.

Angry shouts could be heard in the background. National Guardsmen filled in the screen, carrying clubs and guns. Wind tousled Ricardo's dark hair as he spoke into the microphone.

Not a word he said penetrated her consciousness. Suddenly she felt an overwhelming desire to offer him protection, a haven filled with safety and peace.

A blaring commercial broke onto the screen and Angela realized Ricardo's report had ended. Confused and upset, she stood and began to pace. Her problem was more serious than she'd thought. She cared about Ricardo's safety, yet mistrusted him in her class. She respected his decisive action as a reporter, but one of those decisions could involve discrediting her as a teacher. Expertise in the field of education gave her professional confidence. But she had no defense against the physical attraction she felt toward Ricardo. How was she going to survive this month?

RICARDO PACED the small area in front of the counter in the school office. Where was Angela? He and Ken needed time to set up before the students arrived. Besides, he wanted a few moments alone to talk to her. It wasn't that he had anything to say in particular. He just wanted to hear her voice. See her smile.

The door opened and a woman walked in carrying a small child and leading another. She glanced at Ricardo and then at the bouquet of flowers he held in his hand.

Ricardo's grip tightened around the wrapped stems. The flowers had seemed like a good idea on the way over here. A gesture of friendship. Now he felt foolish. He forced himself to ease his hold. If he didn't relax, the bouquet would be as mangled as the flower little Juan had brought Angela the first day Ricardo had visited.

The door opened again and Ricardo sighed with relief. The sight of Angela blocked out the sounds of the other voices in the office. His whole attention focused on her—the way the light shone on her white-gold hair, the way the folds of mauve jersey clung to her body, the way her perfume wafted into the room.

"Sorry I'm late." She didn't smile but fumbled in her purse for keys. "The traffic this morning is unreal. My bus was late and I missed my connection. I had to wait for the next one."

Ricardo nodded, trying to shake off the feeling that she was using the traffic as an excuse. In fact, he had the distinct impression that she wished to avoid him altogether, especially since she kept averting her eyes.

"Ken's in the lounge. I'll go get him so we can set up our equipment."

"Fine. I'll go on ahead and open the door."

She started to move away but Ricardo blocked her exit. He spoke in low tones, holding out the bouquet of spring flowers. "Will these make you smile?"

She glanced up but there was no warmth in her eyes. Only wariness. "Thank you." She took the bouquet without touching his fingers.

Ricardo waited for a few minutes after she left the office and hurried down the hallway toward her room. He tried to ignore his feelings. It wasn't possible that such a small rejection could hurt. Maybe it wasn't even a rejection. She was probably nervous about filming today. Trying to hold that thought in mind, Ricardo went in search of Ken.

After an hour in the classroom, Ricardo realized Angela had had reason to be nervous. He was a wreck, himself. He directed his cameraman to close in on the two students sitting on the floor in one corner of the room. The strain he'd been under, and physical danger he had been in in Copperville, were nothing compared to the stress caused by this class of innocent six-year-olds.

It wasn't the students who made him tense; it was their teacher. Angela—he wanted to strangle her slender neck. Two weeks. He had been gone two whole weeks. Surely she could have pulled the class together enough to give some semblance of order for his visit today. How the hell was he going to make this chaotic mess look good? With reluctance he bent down to place the microphone where he could hear the students.

"No, Juan," little José said quietly but firmly. "Voltron *is* fighting the Robeast."

Great! Just what Angela needed—kids fighting—and she sat over there at her table, oblivious to it all.

"But you can't just have fighting in your story," Juan insisted while he jabbed a finger on a paper full of scribbles. "Remember what Teacher says—you have to have a problem."

"I will have a problem," José assured his friend. "Voltron is going to get trapped."

"Con permiso," Ricardo could not help interrupting. "Why do you need a problem in your story?"

"It won't be interesting." The boy didn't bat an eye. The fact that an adult, and a stranger at that, had questioned him didn't faze him in the least. He spoke with the authority of experience. "If you don't have action and conflict, there's no story."

"You sound like my boss," Ricardo commented with ironic surprise. He listened in disbelief as the boys worked more on plotting. They knew the elements needed to make a story work. Angela had explained that reading quality literature to the students would teach elements of story. He hadn't believed it at the time, but he could see the evidence before him. It would help Angela's case—at least somewhat.

Ricardo looked around the room. More students sat in small groups, talking. In the corner sat three children coloring pictures with bright felt-tip pens. His crew members were taping the other conversations. Unfortunately, they would show students visiting and playing instead of working.

Frowning, Ricardo regarded Angela. Every now and then she glanced up to survey the class, but never did she correct the behavior of her students. What could he do to get through to her?

A loud clatter drew his attention to Ken. A chair had toppled where a microphone cord had caught it. Lisa, the girl who had been at Angela's apartment that day, righted the piece of furniture.

"It's okay," she assured Ken. "Teacher says when we make mistakes, we learn."

Ken flushed a bright red under his freckles. Ricardo laughed, enjoying Ken's discomfiture. He'd seen Ken remain cool and collected in the slums of Los Angeles and during the riots in Copperville. The fact that a mere six-year-old could unnerve his most enterprising cameraman renewed his flagging sense of humor.

He glanced at Angela, expecting to share the irony. His expression sobered when he encountered her ice-blue gaze. What had gotten into her?

At first he had excused her cool attitude as nervousness because of the camera. But as each minute passed, he grew more certain that she directed those freezing glares at him purposefully. What had happened to change her attitude? When he had left her, that day at the pool, she had been warm and receptive.

Angela had been in his thoughts constantly over the past two weeks. Still, he needed to be objective in his relationship with her—at least until the end of this month.

He observed Angela as she worked with a student. The bouquet of flowers sat in the middle of the table. At least she'd put them in a vase. There was no reason for her treating him like her enemy. When class ended, he promised himself he'd get to the bottom of it.

Ricardo moved on to another group of students. Three were standing by a table that contained cartons of labeled plants.

"My plant's bigger."

Ricardo picked up the voice of a blond-haired girl named Ana.

"No, it's not," the second insisted in Spanish.

The third girl ran over to Angela's desk and began rummaging through its contents. Ricardo's immediate reaction was to reprimand her, but he paused and turned to see Angela watching him. Stepping back, he waited for her to finally scold one of her students.

To his amazement, she nodded to the girl and refocused her attention on the student beside her. Ricardo couldn't control his need to interfere another minute. He strode over to Angela. With satisfaction he noticed how her muscles tensed at his approach.

"Do you always let your students have the run of the classroom?" he whispered with a touch of sarcasm.

She looked up, startled at his question. "It's their classroom, Mr. de la Cruz."

Mr. de la Cruz, he mimicked to himself. Such a show of cold formality. He wanted to grab her shoulders and shake the haughtiness out of them.

"They're going through your desk," he pointed out. Never had he seen a student allowed near the sacrosanct drawers of a teacher's desk—let alone inside them.

"Go back and observe, Mr. de la Cruz." She smiled but it didn't reach her eyes. "You might learn something about what they're doing."

Her reminder of his duty annoyed Ricardo. He returned to the girls, barely restraining his flash of temper.

"*Aqui esta*. Here it is." The girl at Angela's desk held up a ruler in triumph.

Ricardo eased closer as the students began measuring the plants. The act in itself did not merit particular attention, but what followed had him intrigued.

"Mine is twenty-two centimeters and yours only nineteen," the blond girl informed them with an I-told-you-so attitude.

"What soil is yours in?" the other girl asked, not at all daunted by the other's triumph.

"Potting soil," Ana answered.

"It must be better than sand. Mine's in sand and Ana's is in clay," the dark-haired girl observed.

"Let's get our notebooks." Ana jumped up in the air with excitement.

The girls ran to their desks and grabbed three-ring binders and pencils. He sighed in dismay while the girls crawled under the table to write on the lined paper. Dismay turned to interest when he noticed the data the girls wrote in their notebooks. Not only did they record the size of the plants but they included comments on why each plant had its own respective height.

Were these youngsters applying the principles of critical thinking at their age? He didn't think it possible, yet the report Angela had given him to read claimed children in our schools were seriously lacking in critical ability. Was Angela right? Was it the system? Angela claimed the "holistic" approach produced incredible results, but this was too much. They must be from the "gifted" program.

So the day went, chaotic and incoherent. On the positive side, the students were happy and content—but who wouldn't be, with the run of the class that they had? On the negative side, who could tell? As far as he could see, too much time was wasted running around the room. The students should be sitting at their desks working in math books or reading.

The confusion muddled his objectivity—or was it Angela's distant manner? Looking back on the day, all he could think about were her expressionless features. His only consolation was that there hadn't been smiles for her students, either.

Perhaps the taping had unnerved her more than he'd expected. Well, he would soon find out. Until he had this dissension between them cleared up, he wouldn't be able to make head or tail of what he'd observed today.

Where do they get their energy? he wondered, watching the last affectionate student hugging her goodbye. She looked exhausted. He knew how she felt.

"I'm beat," he admitted.

"They have a million questions, don't they?" she agreed with a smile.

Ricardo responded to it with surprising eagerness, his attitude softening.

"They want to know everything—right now." He chuckled.

"At least you and Ken are giving them on-site knowledge of behind-the-scenes television." The hint of sarcasm cut through his lowered defenses.

Her reserved manner back in place, she strode over to her desk to stack the notebooks scattered across the top.

Ricardo followed. "We need to talk."

"I can't." She looked up, a flicker of regret in her eyes.

"Can't or won't?" he countered, annoyance flaring again.

"I have a meeting I must attend." She reached for her keys and walked to the door. "The door is locked, Mr.

de la Cruz. Please close it when you and Ken are through."

Frustrated, Ricardo watched as she left the room. He went over to Ken, who was packing his equipment in the large black cases. He helped his cameraman finish up, vowing to himself that, today, Miss Angela Stuart would not have the last word.

ANGELA PARKED HER white Plymouth sedan in the car-port behind her apartment. Due to the late hour of the meeting, she had taken her car.

"What a day!" she exclaimed with heartfelt relief that it was over.

She rested her forehead against the steering wheel. She'd had stressful days before, but today had topped any of her previous experiences.

Ricardo de la Cruz. Images of him challenged and tormented her, and there were four sessions left to go!

Resolving not to let defeat creep in, Angela exited her car. A soak in the apartment-complex whirlpool tub would help clear her mind. The promise of relaxation added a slight spring to her step. The flowers in the courtyard scented the late-evening air. Angela took a deep breath, letting the peace and quiet restore her spirits.

"Must have been a late meeting." Ricardo's voice emerged from the vicinity of her front door.

A rush of anticipation came and went as she watched him walk toward her. What did he want now?

"Maria and I went out to dinner after the meeting," she explained. "Are you waiting to see me?"

"I want to talk."

She paused, eyeing him with an expression of disbelief. "I've scheduled our conference for our last session."

"There are some things I'd like you to explain."

"About today?"

He nodded. Angela called on her last ounce of energy. After all, it was important that Ricardo understand the whole-language program and what she was doing in the classroom. "Come on in, then. I'll try to answer your questions."

His steps brought him close to her—*too* close. It would be so easy to lean against him and breathe in the musky scent of his skin.

Angela started to back away. Taking a step sideways, he let her pass and then followed her into her apartment.

"This won't take long," he promised, shutting the door behind him.

"Since you insist on talking with me, Mr. de la Cruz, you may as well have a seat." The haughtiness in her voice chilled him. She refused to offer him a drink although she could have used one herself to stop the trembling.

He sat down on the sofa, sprawling his long legs in front of him. His apparently relaxed pose didn't fool Angela for a minute. She sat in the curved section opposite, and wished that the black table between them was larger.

"I want to know why you're acting like I have the kiss of death." He didn't waste time with formalities.

"An appropriate choice of words." She managed to control a shudder that would have revealed her apprehension.

"Why?"

Angela refused to acknowledge the hurt in his voice. "I think your intention to discredit me warrants that attitude."

"I'm not out to get you. I want to help you, Angela."

"I don't need help. I need understanding and an open mind. I saw you watching those kids. You only saw them running around and talking and—"

"They *were*," he interrupted, gesturing in frustration.

"But did you hear what they said?"

"Of course. Two of your boys were giving each other a rather impressive critique of their stories."

"They've been taught to give input and help each other revise," she elaborated, relieved that he recognized what the students were doing.

"It sounded good, Angela, but I looked at the kid's paper. All he had on it were scribbles."

"He's writing his way, which means he can still participate in thinking even though he can't write alphabetically. At his stage of handwriting development, the function is more important than the form."

"You mean that was his work?" His dark eyes widened.

"He'll figure out the plot with his friends and finally with me. I edit and type his story, he illustrates it, and voilà, he's published a book."

"That's crazy!" Ricardo exploded, the outburst lifting him out of the sofa to tower over her. "How can you edit and type his story when you can't even read it?"

Angela remained undaunted by his outburst. "It's simple. He reads the story to me and I write the standard words below his invented words. When I type the story for his book, I correct the grammar."

"Doesn't that upset his ego?"

"No. They realize they don't use standard spelling. They also appreciate being able to publish a book when they've composed it."

"He can't read or write and you tell me he's published a book."

"We have our own class publishing company and we make a big deal about them ending as finished copy."

"Angela, we aren't playing games here. Those kids have to learn how to read."

"They do, Mr. de la Cruz, better than the average first-grader, actually."

"I don't see how, when—"

"You will," she interrupted with a touch of impatience. "That's what we plan to explain. But our explanations aren't going to have any meaning to you if your mind is already set."

That threw him. He was renowned in his work for being fair and astute. "Angela, I'm trying to understand, but it's all very strange."

"Trust me. After we explain the theory, it'll become clear."

He slumped down on the velvet cushions and, bracing his chin on his steepled fingertips, he brooded.

"I don't want the rest of our time taping to be like today," he told her. Sincerity traced a furrow across his brow. "You're upsetting my cameraman, as well as your class."

"You're right." She leaned back, defeated. "The students sense my hostility."

"There's no need to be hostile toward me." Soft promise edged his tone. "I don't want to hurt you."

The strange part about it was, she believed him. Perhaps Cathy and Lupe had misunderstood his intentions. After all, he did plan to spend several days in her classroom. That had to look suspicious to them. Then, too, if she was honest, she'd admit there was a possibility that the two had deliberately lied to upset her. Even though the two teachers enjoyed giving her a rough time, it was hard to believe they'd go this far— not with an influential man like Ricardo. Then again...

"Do you have more questions about what you saw today?" she relented.

"Quite a few." He smiled then. "But I'll wait until the conference you've scheduled. You're tired."

The warmth of his smile washed over her and she relaxed. "I don't mind if—"

"Later," he interjected as he stood to leave. He reached over and took her hand to pull her up with him. "If I assure you I haven't closed my mind or set any opinions, will you promise me we won't have any more icy glares?"

"I promise." For the first time that day, she gave him a genuine smile. She noticed how his tension eased. It surprised her that she had the power to upset him.

"Till next week." He traced his finger along the line of her cheek.

Her eyes closed in response to his touch. When she opened them, he was gone.

5

THE NEXT TWO SESSIONS proceeded without hostile tension. Ricardo and Ken relaxed and the students reacted to the camera with less caution. Once again Angela began to enjoy her students.

At one point during the third session, her glance came to rest upon Ricardo. Attentive and alert, he was listening to Carlos. They sat on the carpet, two dark heads, the small one bent over to read, the larger, powerful head cocked to hear the child's story. Angela smiled to herself. If Carlos was reading his latest space fantasy, Ricardo would have a surprise in store for him.

"*Maestra*." The high-pitched voice brought her attention back to the child at her side.

"Read me your story, Leticia."

Angela listened with half an ear as the little dark-haired six-year-old read. A loud guffaw interrupted Leticia's words and both looked up to see Ricardo, head thrown back, rocking with laughter.

"That's the funniest story I've heard in a long time," Ricardo told Carlos, giving him a pat on the back.

"Carlos always writes funny stories," confirmed one of his friends.

Several students had edged over to the pair still seated on the floor. Curious and always in search of attention themselves, they wanted to be in on the center of activity. For the same reason, Angela stood and joined them.

"You've heard this story?" Ricardo asked one of the bystanders.

The other students, noting his surprise, began to barrage him with plots.

"You have terrific imaginations!" He complimented the group while glancing over at Angela.

She noted his delight. In that instant she realized an essential truth about Ricardo de la Cruz: Under that tough exterior and self-assured attitude hid a sensitive man.

Later, after dropping off the class for their music lessons with the specialist, she tried to appeal to that aspect of his nature.

"You like children, don't you?" she asked him as they returned to her classroom.

"Yes," he answered, but suspicion showed in his eyes when he looked at her.

"They sense your interest. You get along well with them."

"That's because they know where I stand. They realize I'm not going to let them get away with anything. Kids respect that, you know."

His words filtered into her thoughts. Was there a touch of reproach in his tone?

"What's that?" she asked.

"Structure, boundaries, limits." He began to gesture with his hands. "Children need to know the parameters of acceptable behavior, and then those parameters need to be enforced. They don't respect you otherwise."

"I agree," she murmured.

"Do you?" He stopped and placed his roughened hands on his hips. The green grass and the crimson bougainvillea that lined the breezeway faded into the background. The force of the man's physical presence captured her total attention. His next words, however, broke the spell.

"If you believe that, why do you let the children misbehave?" She could see him struggling to understand.

"Who was misbehaving? Everyone was working today—even Fernie."

Fernie had been on his best behavior to impress the "big telebision mans," as he called them. Smiling, she could just imagine the restraint Fernie must have used to control his hyperenergy. Couldn't Ricardo see that and appreciate the effort?

"They were all running around loose again," Ricardo protested, and Angela could hear his frustration.

Movement across the courtyard caught her attention. Lupe and Cathy had been standing watching the exchange between her and Ricardo. *Great.* Now the two would really have something to gossip about. She hoped they were far enough away to be unable to hear what was being said. All she needed was to have Ricardo's criticism bandied about the school. And the two women would see to it that it was.

Annoyed with Ricardo and the whole situation, she swung around and continued toward her classroom. Ricardo looked astonished, but that was too bad. They needed to continue this discussion in private.

On the way, she lowered her voice to be sure Cathy and Lupe couldn't hear. "It doesn't look like it to you because of your preconceived notions, but I run a very strict class."

Her linen slacks swished together with her quick steps. Ricardo lengthened his stride to keep up with her.

"The rules are simple, but enforced. Every child has had it drilled into them that they are at school to *learn* and in class they *work*. If they want to play, I tell them to stay home. If they insist on playing at school, I send them home."

"That's a punishment?" He paced beside her and held open the door.

"To a six-year-old, it's devastating." She entered the room and motioned Ricardo to follow, aware that his glance had raked her from head to toe. Her voice broke. "They love school."

Ricardo's cameraman had retreated to the teachers' lounge for a break, for which Angela was thankful. She didn't want Ken sharing Ricardo's prejudices, nor did she think his awareness of their dissension would help her cause. The respect and loyalty he felt for Ricardo was obvious.

"But how can you tell if they are working or playing?" Ricardo asked before he hooked a leg over a nearby desk and sat down.

The casual action distracted her for a second. How natural he looked, even among the miniature furnishings of the classroom! She could spend all day looking at him.

"There's a distinct difference between the voice tone of children playing and children fighting. Their laughter is different, too, and so are their movements." She smiled as she settled on the top of a desk across from him. He was trying to understand her argument—it was all she could realistically ask of him.

"Experience with kids gives you insight." She shrugged, trying not to notice how the muscles in his leg strained against his slacks. "Just as I imagine experience has taught you how to tell if a person you're interviewing is hiding something or lying."

"I see your point," he conceded, after a long moment of contemplation.

Angela watched, alert to every nuance of movement and tone. His brow furrowed while he rubbed his jaw. His mind must race like a computer—accepting and rejecting data. She held her breath, wondering what it would feel like to run her fingers across his chiseled features.

"Okay. Assuming they're all working and not playing—" He looked at her, his ebony eyes filled with questions and some other, indefinable element. He hadn't accepted her premise yet, but the unusual component of his glance distracted her from the task of convincing him. She had to force herself to listen to his words. "How can they be learning when they work with *each other* instead of with *you*? It's like the blind leading the blind."

Shifting her gaze from the intensity of his, she searched her mind for a sensible answer. "Children learn from each other. They know far more than we give them credit for," she finally managed.

He cast her an indignant scowl, which she ignored. She walked to Carlos's desk. When she realized Ricardo's gaze was focused on her body, she trembled slightly. She shook the fat, lined papers to distract his attention from her and direct it back to the issue. The movement also helped to calm her nerves.

"Look at Carlos's story as an example." She perched next to him to show him the child's work. Awareness of him charged through her body. Her fingers shook as she pointed to the words. "Would you believe that a six-year-old had mastery of such rich language? Look how he sets mood and emotion with these adjectives. You heard the reaction of the class."

"Yes, but—"

"First-grade preprimers don't use words like this," she interrupted him. "They use one-syllable flat vocabulary that says nothing—and do you want to know why?"

Caught up in the conviction of her beliefs, she missed the gleam of amusement in his eyes.

"Why?" he asked as his breath fanned her cheek.

Distracted, she peered at him and saw the humor lurking at the curves of his mouth.

"Because." She stood, miffed that he found her speech entertaining, and disturbed because he could fluster her with a sensual look. Determined to convince him, she continued. "They think six-year-olds don't know any complicated words yet. So they stifle and bore children with subhuman language."

"But if they can't read—"

"That's the whole point," she interrupted and threw her hands in the air for emphasis. "They aren't going to *want* to read when there's nothing meaningful in the content of the books."

"I admit your students want to read, but *can* they?"

"It's hard to believe, but most of these first-graders *do* know how to read and write. What's more, they do so at a level way above their grade level."

With a sweep of her hand, she grabbed several books published in class from the bookcase. "Look at these. They were written by the children, using their language, telling stories that mean something to them." She paused for effect and took a deep breath. "They can read these."

He thumbed through the pages while avoiding her eyes. "Of course, they can read these. They've memorized them."

"But, don't you see?" She tapped a coral nail on the large print. "Through *familiar* language they figure out the written system. It's like learning how to talk. You listen to language around you and from what you know, you generalize and expand your vocabulary. It's the same premise here."

"That doesn't make sense." He set down the books and grabbed Carlos's papers. Angela couldn't take her eyes off his blunt-tipped fingers. "Look at this kid's writing. Who's going to teach him to spell, use proper punctuation and grammar? You need to teach him that."

"I do." She focused on his words in disbelief. Did he actually think she sat doing nothing all day? "When they are ready, they bring me their work and we conference and edit. That's what I do at the table."

"But it's only *one* child."

"It is hard to get to all of them when I have such a large class—I admit that." She began to pace, forgetting about the disturbing quality of the man as her defenses rose.

A strand of hair fell across her face and in an unconscious gesture she brushed it back with her hand. The action pulled her loose-fitting coral blouse against her breasts. When she turned to face Ricardo, she caught the admiration in his glance. A thrill raced through her, but she suppressed her reaction. She had to persuade Ricardo that the children did in fact learn more through this "holistic" approach.

"When I do get to that child, he learns what I teach him because it's relevant to what he needs *at that mo-*

ment, for *his* work." She began to pace again, this time conscious of his gaze following her every step. "When a teacher stands in front of the class and lectures, maybe the child learns, and maybe he doesn't. He might not even be listening. You have no way of knowing."

"But at least you know you taught it." He stood and blocked her path.

"Did I, though?" She stared up at the face looming above hers, willing him to understand and ordering her senses to ignore him. "If they don't *need* to learn it, they won't. So I've wasted my time and theirs."

"But most of them probably will."

"I can't gamble with their minds. My way tells me they *did* learn what they need to know." In protest, she placed the palm of her hand on his arms. "They want the information. They use it and internalize it. Don't you see how essential that is?"

Tanned fingers reached up to cover hers and press her hand closer. The warmth from his skin penetrated the smooth fabric of his plaid sport shirt.

"Angela," he murmured.

All arguments in defense of her teaching vanished. Awareness that she was even a teacher disappeared.

For several minutes, Ricardo hadn't heard a word she had spoken. Oh, he'd been listening and he had filed away her comments for future consideration. But at this moment, all he could think about was . . . fire.

She reminded him of a white-hot blaze. In a flash she would flare up in defense of her students or her teaching. But when he had whispered her name just now, her eyes had been smoldering. Underneath the professional demeanor and the angry defense burned a passion that he wanted to know intimately.

Now was not the moment. Not in her classroom. But watching her move and speak with such fervor disturbed him. He'd wanted to stop her restless motion by pulling her into his arms. His resistance had amazed even him. But when she had placed her slender fingers on his arm, all intentions of propriety and timing vanished. He wanted—no, *needed*—to touch her.

"You drive me crazy," he whispered.

Wrapping his fingers around her hand, he pulled her resisting body closer to his. Her weak struggles were easy to temper until she gave in and stopped inches from him. Not daring to move, he stood still, breathing in the fragrance of her perfume.

"We can't do this." Her voice reached him, breathless and quivering.

"I know. Just stand there—close—for a moment," he promised, giving her hand a gentle squeeze. He wondered if she could hear the way his heart pounded.

"The students . . ." Her voice trailed away.

"Maybe Carlos will whisk us away in his magic spaceship." He heaved a wistful sigh before he let her go.

"It would be our luck that he'd whisk the whole class with us."

"Ugh," he teased. "What a cruel turn of mind you have."

She smiled. The tinge of pink that flushed her skin revealed that she was as disconcerted as he. He reached out a finger to touch her cheek, wanting to feel the heat, but she turned aside and walked toward the door.

"It's time to pick up the students. I'll be back," she assured him.

Stunned by the powerful effect she had on him, Ricardo stood still for a moment. He imagined lazy af-

ternoons beside the pool—the sun would warm their
bodies while the look in her eyes would inflame him.

He began to restlessly move about the classroom.
Traces of Angela were evident everywhere. Why
couldn't he stop thinking about her? Why did he desire
her so strongly?

Other women had never affected him to such an extent. They had attracted him. But they had never distracted him from his work. Whereas thoughts of Angela
drifted into his mind, even while he was immersed in a
story.

That hadn't happened with Yvonne. In the years he
had lived with her, she hadn't invaded his thoughts as
Angela had these past few weeks. Yvonne had been a
reporter and they had decided it unrealistic to marry.
The decision proved wise after Yvonne had received an
offer to anchor a newscast back east. In all honesty, he
had to admit that he hadn't really missed Yvonne—and
especially not now.

Angela had somehow managed to capture his heart
and mind. One smile from her wreaked more havoc
than any woman ever had, Yvonne included.

The door opened and his heart pounded with anticipation. He turned, expecting Angela, only to be
greeted by Lupe Cartenega and Cathy Jones. His gut
reaction to the two women was dislike. He hadn't cared
for the questions they'd asked when they'd stopped by
the news station before his trip to Copperville. Their
interest in his impression of the whole-language program had seemed phony to him. He hoped they didn't
want to talk now.

"Angela's not here," he told them. "She went to the
music room to get her students."

"We know." Lupe, the taller woman, stepped forward. "We came to talk to you."

He groaned inwardly.

"Angela hasn't told us what you've thought about her program."

He was sure she hadn't. He doubted anyone would go around advertising that their teaching methods were suspect. The women were fishing for information, but he wasn't going to be the one to give it.

Lupe looked back at the door and then in a confidential tone asked, "Is Angela being investigated?"

His eyes narrowed as he studied the woman. There was something calculating about her glance. Or was he suddenly feeling protective of Angela?

He stated the obvious: "We're here simply to observe the whole-language methods and tape them."

"Are you going to air them?" Cathy asked.

"I'm not working for the station on this. I told you that before."

"We thought since the video equipment—"

"Which is privately owned," he pointed out. All he needed was for the program director to get on his back.

"Are you doing this for the board?" Lupe asked.

He supposed it would appear that way since he'd been on the board last year. "Look. I'm a concerned citizen, interested in the continuing educational programs. That's all it is."

"We'd be happy to show you our classrooms." Lupe's voice had gone sugary now.

So that was their game. They wanted all the attention for themselves. If they only knew why he was observing Angela so closely, they wouldn't be in such a hurry to invite him in.

"Be sure and come see us," Cathy added as they headed toward the door.

Ricardo gave a noncommittal nod, relieved when they left. He wondered how close they were to Angela. His working relationships with colleagues were tight. But traveling all over the Southwest helped cement the bonds of friendship. Perhaps the working conditions in a school were different.

Yet he'd noticed the closeness between Angela and Maria. He didn't get that feeling with Lupe and Cathy.

Before he could contemplate the matter further, he was interrupted by the return of his cameraman.

"Daydreaming?" Ken paused from adjusting his camera to peer at Ricardo.

"Planning a follow-up story on the Copperville strike for tomorrow's broadcast," he lied, while shrugging his shoulders in a futile attempt at nonchalance.

"She's gotten to you, huh?" Ken gibed with certainty.

"What're you talking about?" Ricardo stiffened, knowing it was useless to hide anything from Ken. They'd worked together for too many years.

"They didn't have teachers that looked like that when I was in school," Ken observed. "And I've seen the way you watch her."

"Lay off." Ricardo scowled at him. The fact that Ken's ribbing was getting to him proved how close to the mark he was.

"Be careful. You're walking a fine ethical line."

Ricardo didn't respond. He knew Ken meant the warning as a friend. They watched out for each other. It had always been that way. Ever since his first investigative report when Ken had been assigned to him and they'd exposed the Simpson Textile Company in East

Los Angeles. It hadn't been hard for Ken to figure there was more involved in it for Ricardo than just a story.

Ken had probed until Ricardo finally admitted his vendetta to avenge his father's death. They'd ended up with an objective report—thanks to Ken's constant probing of his motivations.

He could trust Ken. He wouldn't bring up issues that could damage his reputation—or Angela's. Nor would Ken pass judgment.

"We're not on the job here," Ricardo reminded him. "This is off-the-record as far as the station goes. I'm here as a concerned citizen interested in the schools."

Ken grinned. "Like I said. School was never like this."

Deciding that getting back to business was a prudent course to follow, Ricardo began to explain: "Angela told me during lunch that a group of her students are going to dramatize a story. I want you to film the entire procedure."

"Sure thing." Ken positioned his equipment around the area designated as a stage by Angela. "Is it something special?"

"I'm not sure." He helped Ken adjust the lights. "She said that these students act out a story and then she writes it in sequence on a chart. The kids observe the process and are supposed to learn from watching her do it."

"Sounds fun for the kids," Ken commented.

"But does it do any good?" Ricardo muttered under his breath.

Ken gave him an astonished look. Ricardo squirmed under his scrutiny, knowing he deserved the criticism.

"Here they come," Ken announced.

Ricardo looked up in time to see a charge of thirty bodies approaching. With a quick step, he moved out of the way. Didn't these kids ever slow down?

Ricardo watched Angela direct a small group of nonreaders. The other students were seated in various locations around the room, reading to themselves. He noticed, though, that several of them watched the proceedings instead of reading.

It took ten minutes for the group to decide what characters they wanted in their play, and what the play was going to be about. The children made their decisions with very little assistance from Angela. By now he realized that one of the essential elements she taught them was self-direction. The only involvement they asked of her was to take part in the skit.

"Come on, Miss Stuart," they begged, in their lilting Spanish. "You're biggest—you be the dragon."

She looked up then and gazed at Ricardo with an obvious appeal. Ricardo shook his head. There was a limit to how far he would go with the students—and playing a dragon stretched beyond it.

He could see she was sorely tempted to coerce him. He cast her his most stern look and dared her to try it.

"José would make a great dragon," she relented, and Ricardo breathed a sigh of relief.

"No, no. You, Miss Stuart," Fernie insisted.

From their eager faces, Ricardo could tell that they expected her to participate and that she had done so before. Her look of dismay spoke volumes. She wouldn't let her students down, but clearly she didn't want to perform in front of an adult male audience. Ricardo couldn't control his laughter when she bent down on her knees and slashed her arms about, trying to look fierce. She looked about as threatening as a kitten.

The romping and laughter brought back memories of his childhood. His father used to tussle with Ricardo and his brothers when he returned home from work. Watching Angela play with her students made him long for sons of his own.

Wouldn't his sisters love that, he thought? They had been insisting that Ricardo needed to marry, settle down and have a family. But his work was too hectic and time-consuming now to allow for a stable home-life.

The children squealed with delight. Ricardo was half tempted to join Angela and the children on the floor. Ken's chuckle brought him up short.

Madre mío, he swore to himself. That woman could make him forget everything else but her.

"Save the princess," the children chanted.

It happened so fast, Ricardo couldn't have prevented it if he'd tried. Caught up in the drama, José had grabbed a baseball bat and wielded the club in a pretend attack. But he miscalculated and before Ken could react, José smacked the end of the camera. There was a loud crashing sound as the lens shattered and dropped noisily to the floor. Everyone froze, stunned. A ghostly quiet filled the room and Ricardo glared at Angela.

Angela knew she'd had it now. How much would one of those lenses cost? She groaned aloud, the sound reverberating in the silence.

José's dark eyes widened with fear when he heard it. Angela stepped toward him, automatically responding to the panic she saw on his face. But he moved faster than she. In a flash he dropped the bat and tore past his classmates. The door slammed before Angela could reach him.

She merely glanced at Ricardo, not worrying now about either him or the camera. She had to get to José. "Call Maria! She can take the class to her room."

She rushed out the door, aware that Ricardo was gathering the students around him to keep them away from the broken glass.

6

IT DIDN'T TAKE HER LONG to find José. He'd headed straight for the nurse's office where Mrs. Adams held him against her ample bosom, murmuring comforting words in Spanish. His body shook with sobs.

Angela knelt in front of them. "It's all right, José. It was an accident."

Finally José calmed down. Angela slid into the chair next to Mrs. Adams and explained what had happened.

"*Pobrecito,*" Mrs. Adams said. "Poor little one, you'll be fine now. Miss Stuart wouldn't let those men be mad at you."

"We aren't angry." The softly spoken Spanish words startled all three of them as Ricardo entered the office. It was his turn to kneel in front of Mrs. Adams and José. "You were such a brave dragon slayer and Señorita Stuart was such a fierce dragon."

A smile began to curve across José's face as Ricardo continued to speak. Angela smiled, too, charmed by the gentle way Ricardo was handling José. He'd make a good father, she thought—understanding and fair.

José then shook Ricardo's hand, both agreeing to forgive and forget.

"The school day is almost over. Maybe I'll just take him on home and explain to his mama," Mrs. Adams offered.

Angela agreed, and thanked the nurse for making the trip.

As the nurse and José were leaving, Angela turned to Ricardo. "José will be fine. Mrs. Adams has a way with people. She can smooth over all the touchy situations."

"So I gather. She reminds me of my grandmother," Ricardo said.

"She's everyone's *nana*. The students, the parents and even us teachers go to her with our hurts and troubles."

In fact she envied José now. She'd give anything to be the one going home with someone murmuring soothing words of comfort. It had been a doozer of a day.

"You okay?" Ricardo shifted. For a brief second she fantasized about Ricardo taking her home and easing away the stress of the day. Unexpectedly, he brushed cool fingers against her cheek. His eyes filled with tenderness and his glance caressed her face. Angela smiled.

He smiled back. "Now there's some color. I thought for a minute I'd have to call the nurse back."

Her anxiety revived. Ricardo was the source of it, after all. She glanced at him, wondering if his reassurances to José applied to herself.

"We'd better go across the hall to the office and fill out an accident report. If the school doesn't have insurance for this, I'll cover the cost. José's family won't—"

"Don't worry about it."

Angela noticed his tender expression had been replaced by a frown.

"The camera is insured. Like you said—an accident." His frown deepened as he brushed back a loose strand of her hair. "There's one good thing that came of this."

"Hmm?" She looked into stormy eyes and should have been warned, but the feel of his fingers had entranced her.

"You cannot continue this way. You're going to have to change your teaching methods and bring order to your class. This kind of thing cannot be allowed to happen again."

"How can you say that?" she exclaimed, her heart racing in alarm. "After all that's been said between us, you can still tell me that?"

He grasped her shoulders. "I *have* to tell you that. The way your kids act is unacceptable. It's dangerous," he said with irritation.

"Dangerous?" she retorted. "There's never been anyone hurt in my class."

"Someone could have been, today."

"The children were absorbed in the play."

"Absorbed?" he mimicked. "I'd describe them as unmanageable."

"You're being closed-minded again." Hadn't he observed enough these last weeks to change his opinion? It must be her, personally, that he objected to.

That conclusion dismayed her. He didn't care enough to give her a chance.

"Angela." He stroked her cheek and she jerked away while trying to ignore the tingle his fingers created. "Don't do this. I'm on your side."

"Are you?"

Brushing his hands aside, she backed away. "I have data and research to back up my methods. I'll make you understand," she swore. "Nothing is going to change.

You promised me this month, and we're going to see it through."

"Nothing's so important that you should risk your well-being," he advised.

"Are you saying these children are not important?" She gave him a censorious look.

"These children have never been given a chance. People often assume that because they live in the inner city, are poor and are from Mexico, that they will fail or—worse—that they are stupid. Why, I've—"

"We're not discussing sociology here," he interrupted. "I'm concerned about your class."

"Then look at my class. The students are performing above grade level and defying society's expectations. And do you want to know why?"

"I'm sure you'll tell me." He cast her a wry glance.

"My teaching methods, Mr. de la Cruz. The whole-language approach." His wince pleased her. "These kids are smart. We've just stifled their intelligence by using the wrong methods and materials."

"I thought you disapproved of self-righteous statements," he said sarcastically.

"It sounds conceited, I know." Placing fingers to her throbbing temples, she sighed. Suddenly exhaustion washed over her. "But I'm right and I can prove it."

But could she convince this man? At the moment, it all seemed so overwhelming. The shock of the accident, the emotional turmoil with José, and now this. Tears of frustration spilled down her cheeks.

"You're not going to prove anything like this," he soothed. "You're upset and . . ."

"I will. Those kids need me. There're so few who care to . . ." Her voice quivered and then trailed off as emotion tightened her throat.

He pulled her against him. She tried to pull back, resisting the comfort he offered.

"Stop it," he ordered softly, his voice full of concern.

"Let me go."

He tightened his hold. "You're wrong. I do care for those kids."

The fight went out of her. She sank against his chest and let the tears flow.

"I care, Angela," he murmured into her hair. "For those kids—and for you."

But did he, really? How could she care for a man who didn't recognize her efforts as a teacher? She had to maintain her integrity and purpose, even though she couldn't have his respect. The thought saddened her.

"Don't do this to yourself," Ricardo said as he drew back in order to see her face.

Angela kept her lashes lowered. "I'm sorry." She fought to stop the flow of her tears. "I'd better go back to class."

"No. Rest here a few moments." With one hand pressing the back of her head, he pulled her against him. "We've both had a rough go here. Let's just calm ourselves."

His body shuddered, alerting Angela to the fact that he was as upset as she.

Without realizing it, her arms wrapped around his back. His muscles flexed under her touch. His heartbeat sounded in her ear. She rested her damp cheek on his stubbled skin.

His arms tightened around her. She felt as if she could stay in his embrace forever and revel in being cherished.

"Angela, are you all right?" Mrs. Edwards's voice intruded on her fantasy.

Angela quickly stepped away from Ricardo. She had only been seeking offered comfort, but would the principal think it was more?

"She's had a rough day." The deep tones of Ricardo's voice vibrated in the room as he explained what had happened.

"Oh, my. We'd better file a report."

With reluctance, Angela moved away from Ricardo's side. "If the insurance doesn't cover it, I'll pay for the damage."

"Nonsense." Mrs. Edwards shook her head. "I'm sure it'll be taken care of. Just don't hold your breath, Mr. de la Cruz, because these things do take some time."

"No problem," Ricardo assured the flustered principal. "I already told Angela it was covered."

Further argument became futile when Ricardo insisted they drop the issue.

Resigned, Angela finally agreed. "I should get back to my class," she told them.

"Maria's watching them," Mrs. Edwards reminded Angela.

Angela's head was beginning to ache. What she really wanted was to go home.

As if reading her mind, Mrs. Edwards suggested she do so. "The bell's going to ring in a few minutes, anyway. Maria can dismiss your class."

"It isn't necessary..." Angela began, but Mrs. Edwards insisted.

"You look all done in. What you need is some rest."

"I can't. I took the bus and—"

"I'll take you," Ricardo interjected.

"Good idea," Mrs. Edwards piped up before Angela could protest. "You're always putting in extra hours. You deserve to go home early once in a while."

"She's right, you know," Ricardo said, a crooked smile on his face. "Let's go get your things."

"I'll let you take me home," she conceded, "but I'm going to Maria's classroom first."

A slight movement caught her eye. Lupe was standing behind the counter witnessing the exchange between her and Ricardo. That was all she needed. Quickly Angela opened the door, more than ready to leave.

"Angela—" Ricardo started to protest but Angela cut him off short.

"The class is probably upset about what happened. I need to let the children know everything is okay."

"I'll walk you down, then."

¡Caramba! The woman was stubborn. Walking beside her, he watched the sway of her hips. He could still remember the way she felt against his body.

When they reached her classroom door she paused and said with unexpected humor in her voice, "This could get emotional. Want to wait out here?"

"I can take it." He grinned and followed her in.

The noisy class fell silent when Angela stepped through the door. Angela spoke quietly as she reassured them and let them know they were to stay with Maria until dismissed.

One of the children came flying out from the far corner of the room. She threw herself into Angela's arms so hard that Ricardo feared Angela would fall. He braced her with a supporting hand on her waist while she bent to the small child.

The girl burst into tears of relief and Angela pulled her into her lap while she sat in a nearby chair. Ricardo ignored the I-told-you-so look she cast him while she reassured the child.

He looked around him. The rest of the children were shuffling toward Angela. She noticed the others and opened her arms to them.

"There's nothing to be afraid of. Mr. de la Cruz and I know it was an accident."

The children swarmed around Angela. A million questions poured forth and Ricardo realized she had been right. They needed to see that their teacher wasn't angry.

The students surrounded him, as well. He knelt down. Small arms wrapped around his neck as he held the ones who squeezed close.

Their openness and need moved him. He glanced up and met Angela's gaze. Shared understanding passed between them. One child crawled onto his lap and tugged hard at his neck. Angela tried to keep a straight face at his predicament. The fact that children tugged and pulled on her, as well, saved his sense of dignity. Patience and a sense of humor were definite requirements to have around this many children.

It astonished him that they would be so uncertain of her reaction. Come to think of it, they should be. But Angela's soothing conquered their doubts and fears.

Just as the students began to settle down, Ken came through the adjoining door. Amid the confusion, Ricardo managed to speak over the heads of the children to his friend.

"Did you get the equipment picked up?"

Ken nodded, rolling his eyes slightly, letting Ricardo know the extent of the damage. He'd worry about it later.

"I'm taking Angela home. You can go on back to the station," he told the cameraman.

"I think I'll stick around for a while. Maria might need some help."

The way Ken said it made Ricardo take a close look at him. Did he detect a hint of interest in Angela's attractive teammate? No wonder Ken hadn't protested this favor all month.

"Suit yourself," he advised with a sigh. This project was turning into something neither of them had bargained for.

THE DRIVE TO ANGELA'S passed quickly and in silence in the light traffic of early afternoon. He walked her to the door, preparing for the protest he knew she would make.

"Thanks for bringing me home, Ricardo." She turned to smile goodbye after unlocking her apartment door. "And for being so helpful with everything at school."

"I'm not through taking care of you yet," he informed her as he took her elbow and gently but firmly guided her into the apartment. "I'm staying."

The telltale flush on her cheeks pleased him. So the idea pleased her, too. But he wagered she wouldn't admit it. He won the bet.

"You don't need to stay." She didn't sound too persuasive. "I know you're busy."

He gave her a mock stern look. "Your principal ordered rest. Direct me to the kitchen and while you sit down and take off your shoes, I'll get us something to drink."

"You don't need to wait on me."

"I could lie down with you." He leered at her playfully. He loved it when she blushed.

"Really, Ricardo, I'm fine." She sank down on the velvet sofa.

He knelt in front of her. Grasping a slender ankle he pulled off her shoe. His hand slid partway up her silky calf to brace her foot onto his lap. With firm strokes he massaged the bottom of her foot. Her toes curled around his fingers and a gasp of pleasure escaped her lips. Ricardo watched her reaction with a growing pleasure of his own.

After massaging her other foot he lifted her legs onto the couch. He longed to take off the linen slacks and coral blouse, but he wanted more from a relationship with her than just physical satisfaction. She was the type of woman who wouldn't appreciate fast moves, so he contented himself with observing her beauty.

"You're spoiling me, you know," she warned him as he fluffed up the pillows behind her.

"And you love it," he teased.

"Uh-hmm," she admitted before she closed her eyes.

A lump formed in Ricardo's throat. She looked so inviting, reclining there as if she were waiting for him. He wished that she was his. He cared for the woman.

He cleared his throat. "How about if I make us some iced tea?" Maybe the cold drink would cool him down.

"There's some iced tea in the refridge."

"I'll get it."

Rummaging around in her kitchen, he found the glasses and a tray. He noticed how neatly and orderly she placed her belongings. Funny, he thought, she struck him as highly organized, yet her classroom seemed chaotic.

There were those doubts and criticisms again. He didn't want them interfering with his feelings for Angela. He resented that her job had to come between them.

Ricardo lifted his frosted glass and placed it against his forehead. The cool moisture from the condensation eased his headache. How could he resolve this?

"Find everything?" she called from the living room.

"*Sí.* I'll be right in."

With quick, deft movements Ricardo poured the tea.

"You have a nice place here." His hand shook as he passed her the glass of tea. She glanced up as the ice tinkled against the crystal.

"Angela, we need to talk."

She closed her eyes and took a deep breath. "I'm not changing my mind," she informed him.

"I'm not going to ask you to. I want to understand what you're doing. What you said earlier makes sense. Our schools do have a high rate of failure."

He set his iced tea on the table and rubbed his fingers across his brow.

"The high dropout rate is what prompted me to run for the board five years ago." He looked at her, then continued. "It's especially high for Hispanics, you know."

"Over fifty percent." She shook her head in sorrow. "It's a shame."

Yes, he silently agreed. He had been a dropout himself, a *cholo* hanging around with a street gang. He'd bought into the role of failure. But he'd overcome his low self-esteem and wanted to help others do the same. It wasn't easy, but he was committed to devoting time and energy to improving the education system in the barrio. Just as Angela was, in her own way.

"You really care," he commented—more to himself than to her.

"You stood up to me with your cause today." He knelt in front of her and grasped her hands to emphasize his words. As he did so, he tried not to think about how much he wanted to kiss her. "You showed me, Angela. You opened my eyes to the fact that you may really have hit on something, here."

"Do you understand what it is?" she asked, hopefully.

"I'm trying to." His look willed her to believe him. "I want you to show me—make me understand the validity of your program."

Angela sat up, searching his eyes. Sincerity—and something more—radiated from their depths.

"I'll teach you, Ricardo."

"Is it going to be that difficult? The way you're looking at me, you'd think it was impossible."

Couldn't he tell the look she was giving him was not skepticism but relief—and joy? "No. It won't be *that* hard."

He smiled and her heart melted. Reaching up, he smoothed the crease on her brow.

"You looked as if you weren't sure you could pull it off," he told her.

"I'm not certain. You have to admit you can be hardheaded at times."

"Me?" He rocked back on his heels.

"You." She pressed a finger to his chest.

He grabbed her hand and brought her palm to his lips. "I may be difficult to teach, but I'm easy to love."

Yes. He was teasing about *making* love, but she imagined loving Ricardo would be altogether too easy for her own good. "I doubt I could teach you anything about that."

"I have a feeling you could teach me too much."

"You're probably right. I am an expert," she bantered.

"I want to kiss you, but I suppose we should wait until this is over."

My job. She didn't want to think of it now. In truth she had forgotten all about her position. Ricardo could make her forget everything.

"We have one more session, and then the following Friday is our conference with the professors. After that..." He shrugged, but there was promise in his eyes. He spoke in all seriousness. Another trait she had learned about Ricardo today. He had nerves of steel. Hers on the other hand felt like Jell-O pudding.

"You have a one-track mind," she accused while she backed out of his embrace. A resigned expression settled across her features.

He laughed. "Guilty, I'm afraid. And around you it definitely tracks in the wrong direction." A wry smile creased his cheek as he reached for his glass of iced tea. "So much for getting you to relax."

"Maybe we should watch TV." She pointed to the remote control on the table behind him.

He found the remote and pressed the On button. The television, placed against the far wall in a black lacquer cabinet, came on. The jingle of a pop commercial blared into the room. She grimaced.

"You'd better sit over there," she said, gesturing to a swivel chair several feet from the couch. His nearness would make concentration on the screen impossible.

"Do you think it will do any good?"

She smiled but shook her head. "No. But it'll help."

He sat in the chair and raised his glass in a toast. "One week to go, *querida*."

7

QUERIDA. The Spanish word for "dear one" echoed over and over in her mind. The term was used among close friends but was also an endearment for lovers, and she could all too easily envision Ricardo whispering it in her ear.

She mustn't think about that. It might never happen. But what of his toast? *One week to go.* He might as well have said that he was waiting for her. She shivered with nervous anticipation. What did he plan to do? And how should she react?

All he had to do was cast a sexy look her way and she'd melt on the spot. If he touched her, she would be his.

But she shouldn't allow intimacy between them. Their positions demanded maintenance of a professional relationship. She couldn't face the prospect of another scandal like the one with Steve. She was established in her job, and her life was progressing the way she wanted.... No, she didn't want to jeopardize it all for a few moments of pleasure. Nevertheless, these days her emotions appeared to be overriding her logic.

"She did it!"

Looking across the room she noticed the lights flashing and the music blaring from the television. The young contestant had just won the game show's top award. She looked over at Ricardo.

With his fist raised in the air, it seemed as if he had won instead of the contestant. His competitive spirit compelled him to cheer another's victory.

He turned and their gazes locked. He lowered his arm and with care he glanced away to drain the last of his iced tea. Surely he didn't think that gesture would create a distraction. She held her breath.

He raised his head but she couldn't see his eyes. His thick, heavy lashes prevented her. But when he lifted them, he cast her a look of such desire that she gasped.

"Are you involved with someone else?" he startled her by asking.

An invented involvement would be an easy out for her. Protection. She was about to say yes when his gaze faltered with a hint of what—hurt, disappointment? Angela knew the feeling.

"No," she whispered.

"I'm glad."

"And you? Are you in a relationship?"

He shook his head and stared meaningfully at her. "I'd like to be."

She couldn't move or speak. Her eyes widened and her mouth parted in unconscious invitation.

A sharp intake of breath alerted her to his sudden move to stand beside the couch. Her gaze traveled up the long columns of his legs. She could see his muscles tensing and flexing beneath his slacks.

A bright plaid sport shirt covered his chest, but the open vee of its collar revealed smooth dark skin, drawing her glance upward to a crooked grin and black eyes that glimmered with amusement.

"Do I pass?" He spoke with wry humor. "Do you like what you see?"

She would have been affronted except that she knew he had perused her just as thoroughly.

"You'll do." She smiled. In a rare mood of playful passion, she scooted against the pillows of the couch and patted the spot beside her. He paused for a second and then sat down.

"I'm happy you think so." He cocked his head with pride.

His assurance suddenly overwhelmed Angela. Her smile faded. She was very aware that he could hurt her.

He traced a finger down her cheek but didn't make another move. "You see, I'm very interested in you. You're a remarkable woman."

"I'm glad you approve." She mimicked his earlier response.

He chuckled then, and Angela laughed with him. The doubts faded away with their laughter until they were staring into each other's eyes. Angela knew there was a reason to resist this man—but she couldn't think of it right now.

"I probably shouldn't be sitting here."

"No." She shook her head but knew her eyes said yes.

"I want to kiss you. The television didn't help."

What could she say? *Yes, kiss me? Love me?* Her mouth ached from forcing it shut.

There was too much heat in his gaze. "Do you think we could . . ." He cleared his throat.

"No."

His smile turned rueful. "You're right."

Her fists clenched at her sides as she willed herself not to move, when all she really wanted was to wrap her arms around him.

She struggled to remember all the reasons she should want him to leave her alone, but her desire overruled every argument.

He smiled and gathered her into his powerful arms. With ease, he lifted her across his lap and braced her against his chest. "Let me hold you for a few minutes."

"*Just* hold me?"

"We can try it," he murmured into her hair.

It felt right—too right—to be held by him; his touch was creating havoc in her. She stroked the hard muscles of his chest. Fascinated, she slid her hand upward to curl her fingers around his neck. His pulse throbbed against her palm.

Her upraised arm had exposed her midriff. Ricardo placed a warm hand on the rise of her hip and then settled it at the curve below her breast. His fingers gently massaged her side.

"You're on fire," he commented, almost casually. But Angela knew his body was as tense and rigid as hers.

She closed her eyes as waves of longing rocked her. She needed to tell him that she wanted him, but insecurity kept her silent. She could feel the heat from his body burning her chest. But still his hand remained at her side.

"Tell me that you want me," he murmured.

She looked into his eyes. Within their depths lurked desire and . . . vulnerability.

"Yes, I want you."

He groaned.

Unable to bear the sound of it, she covered his mouth with her fingers. "Don't."

He grasped her fingers in his hand. "Does it bother you that I'm in misery?"

She empathized with him. "I don't want you to hurt."

The sincerity in her voice brought a look of tenderness into his gaze. He placed her hand on his heart. *"Mi corazón,"* he whispered. *"Querida."* He brushed her cheek and then traced her lips with his fingers.

Unable to stand any more of the teasing contact, she ran her fingers through his wavy hair. She stilled his restless movements and offered her lips to his, demanding a kiss.

Wanting to please her, he had tried to move slowly. Now her passion swept him away. He could no longer hold back, and with a groan, he lowered his lips to hers.

His tongue probed her mouth. His fingers trembled as he stroked her breasts. Her quivers made the agony of waiting worthwhile. He tried to be gentle when he kneaded the yielding curves, but his hands shook with the effort.

She moaned and, afraid he had hurt her, he let go and reached around her to press her against him.

"I'm sorry," he whispered into her neck.

"No, I'm okay," she reassured him while she smoothed her fingers across the tense muscles of his shoulders.

"I know I shouldn't have done that, but I had to have one kiss from you."

"It isn't all your fault. I wanted it, too."

But one kiss wasn't enough for her, any more than it was for him.

He pulled back to look at her. Damp tendrils of hair lay across her forehead and splayed out, framing her face. Desire was evident in her eyes—and something else that was undefinable.

"You make me feel so . . ." she confessed in a husky whisper. "It frightens me."

"I would never hurt you," he promised as he brushed back the blond wisps of her hair. Her honesty touched him, yet it evoked his own fears.

With a start, he realized she could too easily break the protective wall that for years he'd buried his inner self behind—a wall so thick that sometimes he didn't know his own true self.

Strangely on the defensive now, Ricardo gently pulled away from her, managing to settle her back on the couch before he stood. His muscles constricted about his heart as he watched her smile fade, to be replaced by a look of confusion.

"We're not ready for this," he told her. Hurt clouded her eyes. He wanted to bend down and hold her, at least clasp her hand, but he dared not touch her.

"We could make love now. We both want to. But where would that leave us?"

"You mean tomorrow at school?"

"Exactly." He jumped at the excuse. "Things are moving much too fast between us. Sex now would make it awkward in front of the camera." That wasn't all of it, but it was what he could tell her now.

Her cheeks flushed with embarrassment. Ricardo could have kicked himself. But as he stood looking at her, he knew how it had happened. She didn't flaunt it, but she exuded a subtle sexuality that invited his caress. His body ached with the pain of wanting her now, this very moment, on the couch, or the floor—anywhere.

"I'd better go." He raked unsteady fingers through hair that she had tousled.

She sat up and reached out a hand for his help to stand. "I'll see you to the door."

"No." He backed away with an exaggerated swagger as false as his composure. "Stay there and rest some more. I know the way."

Before he could see her reaction, he went toward the door. The walls seemed to close in around him and an intense urge to flee hastened his steps.

"Sleep well." He had to turn for one last glance.

"You, too," she called to him.

When he saw the white-gold cloud of hair billowing around her face and the rise and fall of her curves as she breathed, he knew he would never be able to close his eyes that night. The tremulous smile that softened her features promised that a long cold shower was in store for him. And the sooner the better.

THE FOLLOWING WEEK dragged torturously on and on. Every spare minute, he'd wanted to call Angela. Immersing himself in work didn't help. The nights were the most difficult. Memories of her touch would haunt his dreams.

With mixed emotions Ricardo faced their final taping session. The project was almost over and he wanted the day to arrive and be over before he went mad. He dreaded being in such close proximity to Angela. He wasn't sure if he could maintain his professional demeanor.

When their last Monday finally arrived, he found it to be as difficult as he'd imagined. It only took ten minutes in her presence to know it wasn't going to work. His concentration scattered with every sound of her voice, every whiff of her perfume and every glimpse of her face.

All he could think about was the way she'd tasted— so sweet when he kissed her—the magic touch of her hands on his body, and her soft pliancy beneath his fingers. He could only think about how much he wanted her until a discreet cough from Ken or a burst of laughter from a child would bring him back to the job at hand.

He suspected that she was suffering as much as he. Eyes that reflected the turquoise blue of her dress, would cloud with longing whenever he captured her glance. If he came near, she started, or if he spoke, she flushed.

She attempted to alleviate the tension by putting him to work.

"The class is divided into groups," she explained. "Each group has to put their worms in different environments. Could you discuss with this group their expectations, and the procedures they follow?"

"Sure." It sounded sophisticated for a first-grade class, but he was beginning to acknowledge and appreciate their capabilities.

"I'm putting my worms in the refrigerator where it's cold," one child announced.

"I'll put mine by the heater," stated another. "They could die in the cold."

"We won't know unless we try it. Teacher says we have to 'sperment.'"

In seconds, his group commanded his attention. Their predictions of results with the worms were amazingly sound. Their ability to practice the scientific method impressed Ricardo. The process did not last long enough. After the group had recorded their experiments in their notebooks, they proceeded to pursue other projects. Left on his own again, Angela dominated his thoughts.

Again he swore under his breath. How could a woman haunt him so?

"What's the matter?" Smirking, Ken came over to stand beside him. "Your mind's wandering."

"That obvious?"

"The two of you—" he nodded toward Angela "—have this room steaming."

"Drop it, Ken," he warned his colleague.

Ken backed off in a hurry. "Okay, okay. Haven't seen a thing."

Ricardo rubbed his fingers across his forehead. It was only ten o'clock. They'd been here half an hour and the tension had them all on edge. He resented it. Besides that, he knew he couldn't continue like this.

"Stay here and tape the rest of the day," he ordered Ken as he decided to leave the strained atmosphere of the classroom and return to the station.

Distance didn't help. He buried himself in projects at the television station but by four o'clock, he found himself gunning the powerful motor of his Ferrari in front of the modern-looking school.

There'd been a lot of changes over the last five years. He took pride in having been part of the governing board that had demanded new buildings. Of course, he hadn't agreed with everything they had decided. Still, he was impressed with the status of the school facilities. If only their problems of curriculum were as easy to solve. The district had several innovative programs operating. He thought of Angela's class and how hard her students worked.

"What happened to you?" Angela's voice startled him.

"Something turned up. I had to return to the station."

"Anything wrong?" she asked.

"No," he said evasively. "Ken gave me the tape of what I missed."

"Will you go over it later?"

"Tonight," he promised as he patted the cassettes beside him. He watched relief replace the concern on her face.

"Can I drive you home?"

"Thanks. It's been a long day."

"Maybe I can do something about that." Ricardo reached across the seats to open the door for her. "We could go to my house. I have a Jacuzzi tub."

"Sounds wonderful." She sat down and her perfume wafted toward him. "But not tonight. After what happened between us, I don't think it would be a good idea to be together." She leaned against the headrest, a frown marring her features.

So, the tension had disturbed her, too. She probably guessed why he'd left.

"Will you spend the weekend with me?" His impulsive request astonished him as much as it did her. "We'll take it slow," he added quickly. He wouldn't want her any other way.

"I'd like that." She smiled at him. Doubt lingered in her eyes, so he didn't give her a chance to say more.

"After the meeting on Friday," he specified. "Sure you don't want to reconsider and come home with me now?" he teased with a sexy grin.

"I'm sure." She laughed.

"Friday, then," he confirmed. As he drove, he imagined rearranging his daily schedule to pick her up and take her home with him every day, where he could massage away the day's hassles, soothe her tensions with a hot whirlpool bath.

When this is over, he promised himself. He watched her walk away from him toward her apartment and didn't feel too disappointed. Friday was only four days away.

ON FRIDAY MORNING, Angela was less tense than she had been for a while. With the professors coming at one o'clock, she needed to be calm. They deserved her best efforts in return for the time and energy they had contributed to the development of the whole-language program.

Looking around the conference room that afternoon, a feeling of satisfaction filled her. Confident that Ricardo would now fully understand her goals, she introduced the university staff.

"Each professor represents a part of the curriculum," she explained to Ricardo. "But math, science and social studies are all integrated with the reading and writing processes to make up a 'holistic' approach.

"We don't teach each subject separately—you know, math for an hour, science for an hour, and so on." She began pacing at the head of the table, her high heels clicking on the hardwood floor. "We try to integrate all of the subjects into a meaningful whole."

"You need to clarify what exactly you mean by 'whole,'" Ricardo interjected.

Angela studied Ricardo, staring into his jet-black eyes. His expression didn't waver but held firm. For a moment she envied him his calm demeanor. Could she maintain her own composure?

"Take, for example, the concept of environment we're studying." She gestured with her hands as enthusiasm for her subject built. "That has usually been a science or social-studies unit. We've used it as both."

"But as you've seen from the students' work," Dr. Wheeler spoke up, "she has also included math, writing and reading within the unit."

"Remember the girls measuring their plants?" Angela jumped back into the discussion. Surely he would relate to this. "They also wrote their data in their notebooks and they read books and magazine articles about plant life because they wanted to understand what was happening."

"Traditional classes read articles, write answers and measure," Ricardo pointed out. "I don't see much difference."

Puzzled, Angela studied Ricardo. Surely he'd observed the process. They'd even discussed it at length. "These students do it individually. They search the information for their own use rather than as a directed reading assignment."

"If the teacher doesn't assign the work, how do you know they read the necessary material?" he questioned.

Willing herself to be calm, Angela took a deep breath. Again Ricardo's attitude puzzled her. For someone who had insisted he possessed an open mind and willingness to be objective, he was acting annoyingly obtuse. What kind of game was he playing?

"If you noticed there are at least a hundred books, magazines or pamphlets on the different aspects of environment that we're studying. The students use them to find answers to their questions."

"That still doesn't mean a *child* will read them."

For a brief moment, when he rubbed his fingers against his forehead, Angela thought he might be suffering from a headache. Maybe that was why he was questioning every practice. But the cool stare he leveled at her made it clear he knew exactly what he was doing.

Her suit made her feel professional but wasn't helping her confidence as much as she hoped when she chose to wear it this morning. Only her conviction in her beliefs could really do that.

"The children are participating in activities, Mr. de la Cruz." She tried to put ice in her voice. "Their interest motivates them. In the case of their plants, they wanted to find information on why they grew or died."

"How can you be sure they're understanding what they read?" He rapped out the question as if he had a whole battery in store for her.

"By their conversation and by the notes they take."

Each loaded question Ricardo asked fueled her anger. If he asked another, she would explode.

Looking around her at the supportive faces of her colleagues, she struggled to defuse her temper. But it didn't work.

"Would you excuse us for a moment?" she asked the group. "I need to confer with Mr. de la Cruz in private." She cast a cool glance at Ricardo. "Shall we?" She gestured to the door.

Ricardo preceded her through to the corridor. Before she could follow, Dr. Wheeler grasped her wrist.

"You're doing fine," she assured her. She looked up to see the others nodding their assent. Their confidence in her boosted her flagging morale. She smiled before she followed Ricardo out the door.

8

CLOSING THE DOOR behind her, she stepped into the hall and in front of Ricardo.

"What are you trying to do to me now?"

Angela stood with hands on her hips, aggressive and on the attack.

"You were the one who set up this conference," Ricardo defended himself.

"And you agreed to cooperate."

"I'm here." He looked truly puzzled, but Angela didn't let that fool her one bit. Ricardo de la Cruz was much too clever and manipulative to be confused.

"And I'm wondering why." She shook her head. "You don't appear to be hearing a word I say."

"What are you talking about?" He reached for her but Angela stepped back.

"You know very well, Ricardo de la Cruz. Every point I make, you argue with. You sound as if you don't believe I know what I'm doing in that classroom. You know better—you've seen me."

She almost shouted the last statement.

"Angela, Angela." He stepped forward in a swift motion to capture her shoulders in his hands.

She fought against the arousal his touch created and scowled at him. "Don't touch me."

"I'm trying to help you."

"Great help. You doubt every statement I make."

His next move startled her. He placed his hands in his pants pockets, rocked back on his heels and burst out laughing. Shocked, Angela stared at him.

"Is that what's bothering you?" He chuckled. "Don't you see what I'm doing?"

"You're trying to discredit me," she accused.

"No." He reached for her, but again Angela side-stepped him. He could charm her into believing anything if he touched her. "I'm playing devil's advocate. If you present the whole-language process to the public, they're going to raise the same questions I have."

He was right. She could picture her school board doing so. Did Ricardo plan to present this to the board, after all?

"I need to see that you can defend yourself," he reasoned. "I need layman's explanations for what I saw. I spent four days in your room and I saw what your students could do, but I need to comprehend the theory behind your success."

She looked at him then, searching the depths of his eyes for the truth of his words.

"Do you understand now?" he asked. Reaching out, he placed his hand on her arm. When she didn't pull away, he slid his fingers down to capture hers.

Angela held on as if to a lifeline. "Ask your questions," she told him. She took a deep breath to strengthen her bravado. "I'll do my best to clarify our position."

"That's all I want."

Footsteps sounded in the hall. Angela glanced up to see Cathy Jones approaching the two of them. Quickly she pulled her hand from Ricardo's, but the way the woman stared at Ricardo's hand, Angela knew she'd seen.

"I thought you were in a big meeting this afternoon." Cathy raised an eyebrow.

There was no reason for Angela to feel uneasy about Cathy's question, but she did. "It's still going on."

"Is Mrs. Edwards still in there?"

Angela nodded, disliking the way Cathy's gaze traveled speculatively between her and Ricardo. "Do you need to talk to her?"

"It can wait. I'll see her later. Lupe and I need to discuss some plans with her." Her voice turned sugary. "After she's finished with you."

Impatiently Angela shifted toward the door of the conference room. "We've got to get back. Excuse us."

Ricardo guided her back inside, where all eyes were riveted on the two.

"Just a meeting of the minds." She smiled, trying to ease the situation.

"More like a clash," quipped Dr. Wheeler. "Bound to happen when two people as strong and determined as you two collide."

Ricardo laughed, genuine appreciation of good humor lacing his tone. "She is imposing."

"Don't we know it," the science professor added with good-natured regret. "We've had several rounds with her ourselves defending our theories against her practical knowledge."

"Which is what I'd like to ask you about." Ricardo brought the discussion back to base with his expertise as an interviewer.

For the next two hours they reviewed the edited tapes and discussed the theory behind each scene. The professors backed Angela with research data. Mrs. Edwards assured Ricardo of the positive reaction from parents. Angela drew on knowledge she wasn't even

aware she had acquired to respond to the continual
barrage.

Ricardo's questions were pointed and astute. Now
that Angela no longer felt threatened by them, she
could see how they revealed the theory and basis for her
methods. Her respect for him rose another notch.

She smiled and continued.

"The students' high achievements are partly due to
their teachers' expectations. Just as we know all children will learn to talk, we *know* that they can read and
write. We don't limit them by assuming that because
they're Spanish-speaking or because they live in the
barrio, they won't succeed." She turned abruptly and
faced Ricardo. He shifted in his chair as if caught daydreaming. Surely he was listening intently.

Dr. Wheeler added, "I see students all the time in
other schools who don't try because they don't believe
they can succeed."

"I've been in classes," another professor spoke out,
"where students are continually told by their teachers
that they're in the 'low' group or the 'slow' group."

While the professors continued to debate, Angela
studied Ricardo, wanting to trace her finger along his
jaw. Then he looked up, and their glances met. A cough
brought her up with a start. She tore her eyes away from
him and gazed at Dr. Wheeler.

"I can see your point," Ricardo interjected. "But how
can we alter ingrained beliefs about failure?"

Dr. Wheeler responded and Angela smiled in thanks.
In her opinion, that represented the primary advantage of the whole-language method. After Dr. Wheeler
finished, she leaned toward Ricardo for emphasis and
spoke in an excited voice. "Success and pride in their
work motivate them to want to learn more."

Ricardo sat back, enjoying the sight of Angela's enthusiasm. In spite of exhaustion that had etched tiny lines around her eyes, they sparkled with animation.

He wondered how secure she was personally. He had the feeling that she wasn't so self-assured in her intimate life. He longed to find out.

Shifting in his seat, he tried to concentrate on her words. It was too easy to be distracted by the movement of her moist lips, her hand gesturing in emphasis and the flowery fragrance that drifted his way whenever she moved.

"Use of their own language and experiences encourages pride of their culture and position in society."

Dr. Wheeler cleared her throat and Ricardo swiveled around to face her. As she remarked, "You ought to appreciate that, being Hispanic yourself."

He remembered the shame he felt because of his accent, and his determination to rid himself of it. Although he loved his family, he still had been deeply ashamed of his Chicano heritage.

If he had grown up proud of his heritage, he might not have built such a wall around his inner feelings. Yet that toughness had brought him to where he was today. Obtaining fluency in English and knowledge of "the system" had been absolute essentials.

"The students *need* to learn English," he said with conviction.

"That is definitely encouraged," Angela assured him. "And they do learn English. But they do so with pride in being able to speak two languages rather than being embarrassed that they speak Spanish."

Suddenly the image of an English teacher he had had in his freshman year at the university came to mind. She had spoken similar words. Due to her influence and her rejuvenating of Ricardo's lost sense of pride, he'd set out in a new direction toward a successful career. Her counseling had encouraged Ricardo to enter the field of journalism. Yet, in all these years, he'd never before given the credit to that instructor. When he thought about it now, he could see how her true dedication had been a major influence in his life. Angela was such a teacher—one who would affect others in a similar way.

Ricardo appreciated the quality that drove her to care for her students. His admiration for her generous and giving nature grew the more he knew her. She had his respect and friendship—elements that, for the first time in his life, he felt, were essential to his interest in a woman.

BY FIVE, everyone in the conference room was exhausted. Ricardo felt as if he'd been blitzed with a full college curriculum in the space of a few hours. In fact he supposed he had been. Rubbing the back of his neck he stood to stretch his legs, stalling for a moment to gather his thoughts before presenting the anxious group with his reaction.

All eyes—tired, yet attentive—were upon him. But he was only aware of Angela's gaze. He looked at her and smiled.

"What you've discussed today, in combination with my observations of Angela's classroom, has been impressive."

Several sets of shoulders, including Angela's, sagged in relief.

Dr. Wheeler spoke up: "It's revolutionizing education, although the system has been slow in accepting it. Students do respond to the whole-language approach.

It stimulates their minds and instills love of reading and research."

When Dr. Wheeler paused, Angela continued: "The main problem, now, is changing the thinking of teachers and parents. We adults are the products of the old, traditional system. It's hard for us to understand how this process can work."

Ricardo reacted defensively at first, but realizing he'd been guilty of exactly what she'd described, he admitted to the group, "I thought I was open-minded about education. I couldn't even see how rigid my ideas were."

"Don't feel discouraged," Dr. Wheeler assured him. "Even we have trouble assimilating it completely."

"It's also why we have so much difficulty implementing the program," another professor added. "Teachers like Angela help us prove what can be done using the whole-language approach."

"Seeing is believing."

The last comment sparked an idea in Ricardo. Perhaps he could be of help. "Would you give me permission to polish the editing on this tape and combine it with a voice-over explanation of your theory?"

Angela's eyes narrowed. "What for?"

He quickly reassured her. "I might be able to devise a tool for you to use in presenting your theory."

Dr. Wheeler spoke up. "We'd want input."

"Of course. Angela can help me and you can preview the film before final print." There wouldn't be any problem finding time to get together with Angela. He'd already planned ahead on that score.

In spite of their exhaustion, enthusiasm spurred the group for another half hour of discussion until, weary but hopeful, they finally adjourned the meeting.

Ricardo went immediately to Angela's side, ready to whisk her away from the others. As far as he was concerned, his so-called private investigation was over. Now he was ready for a personal quest.

Before he could guide Angela away, Mrs. Edwards confronted them. "We need to talk, Angela. I'll call you later."

Ricardo groaned when he saw the puzzled expression on Angela's face. *Don't ask now,* he silently ordered.

The side door opened and the two teachers who'd introduced themselves in Angela's room entered and approached. He groaned again, impatient to leave.

"Lupe, Cathy." Angela acknowledged their presence, her tone oddly strained.

"How'd everything go?" the tall one asked Angela.

"Fine. If you'll excuse us, we were just leaving."

Her chilly tone and abrupt dismissal startled Ricardo. He wasn't going to complain, however. Eagerly he followed Angela as she thanked the professors and then hurried out the door. He guided her to his car.

"What was that last bit all about?" he asked.

"You don't want to know. Talking about those two will make me grumpy and I'm too tired to be even that."

Ricardo chuckled as he helped her settle into the car. She was touchy at this time of day. He'd have to do something to remedy that. All sorts of ideas came to mind.

He slid into the driver's seat and reached across to cup Angela's cheek before starting the engine. "Alone at last."

"And Friday night, at that."

The weekend he'd been dreaming about all week. He'd made dinner reservations, but for a brief moment he was tempted to take her to his home and start right there. *No. First things first.* He put the Ferrari in gear and headed out of the parking lot.

"What did you think of today's discussion?" she asked him as he wove in and out of the Friday-night traffic.

"No, you don't." He cast a critical glance her way. "You promised me the weekend and we don't talk shop on time off."

"But, Ricardo—" she laughed "—I'm dying to know."

Ricardo gripped the steering wheel. From her laughter, he knew she thought he was teasing her. But even if he'd wanted to, he couldn't tell her his response. Besides, he had other things on his mind. "We'll go over it all later, when we view the videos."

"You're serious, aren't you?" she observed.

"Never more so," he assured her. He could feel her studying his profile and sought to distract her. "How does dinner and dancing at The Matador sound?"

"Sure. They serve good Mexican food there."

He preferred to anticipate the weekend awaiting them. As he pulled up in front of The Matador he realized this would be their first intimate time together, and he vowed it would be memorable for them both.

RICARDO SWERVED the sleek Ferrari around the long, curved driveway. He had always admired the elegant grandness of the old mansions along the city's exclusive central corridor. He loved living in the area—even though his house was considerably smaller than those surrounding it, it was built in the same architectural style.

He glanced over at Angela. She sat with eyes closed, leaning her head on the headrest. *Pobrecita*. It had been a rough day for her. Tonight, he would make it all worthwhile. Ricardo's heartbeat quickened with eager expectation. He pulled into the garage, doused the lights and turned to Angela.

"Sweetheart." When he gently drew her close to him, desire hit him in a rush, and he paused, enjoying it.

"Where are we?" She shifted slightly and her fragrance drifted up to tantalize his heightened senses. "I'm so full."

"You ate a huge dinner," he teased.

"I'm always ravenous after I've been nervous," she admitted. "Today just about did me in."

"You aren't nervous now, are you?" he asked.

"No." She nudged her head into the curve of his neck. "Dinner was wonderful."

Her gesture tested his composure. He bent his head and nuzzled the wispy tendrils of hair at her temple.

"Are we at your place yet?" she mumbled before she turned to place butterfly kisses on his neck. The light, feathery touches tested his self-control but not as much as when she captured his lips.

"Uh-hmm." He finally broke away from her. "Let's go."

Shifting her weight from him, he edged out of his side of the car and went around to help her out. He resisted the urge to pull her into his arms right there in the musty garage.

"Are you sure it's a good idea for me to stay here?" She seemed reluctant to follow him out into the flower-scented yard.

"Afraid?" he challenged.

"Maybe." She tilted her chin at a stubborn angle.

"Angela." He pulled her against him and wrapped persuasive arms around her slender curves. She molded against him in automatic response and Ricardo smiled with satisfaction. "It's more private here than at your place. Besides, we won't do anything you don't want to do."

"You can promise me that?" she asked, disbelief edging her sultry tone.

Before he answered, he bent his head to gently brush his lips against hers. It took tremendous willpower not to crush her to him and deepen the kiss. Just the light touch had clenched his insides into a painful knot and sent his heart skittering. He whispered into her parted mouth. "We'll only go as far as you say."

"I don't believe it."

"Ah, but you see, *querida*. I plan to make sure you want it all."

"That sounds promising."

He reached down and, with ease, lifted and carried her outside into the star-laden night. Her smooth arms curled around his neck, sending shivers of pleasure throbbing through his body.

The spring night air wafted around them, and with it, the scent of orange blossoms. Ricardo's footsteps echoed in the night quiet as he followed the walkway of his backyard patio.

He carried Angela into a trellised gazebo at the far end. Honeysuckle vines covered the latticed structure, darkening the interior like a cave. When the lapping of water reminded Ricardo of the nearness of the Jacuzzi, he set Angela on her feet.

"Are your muscles sore from all our dancing?" he asked.

"I couldn't dance another step." She sighed and started to move away from him.

"Careful," he warned while he grasped her easily around the waist. "The Jacuzzi is right here, so don't fall in."

"Is it hot?" she asked.

"Very."

"My feet are going to thank you for this."

Ricardo laughed.

"Take your shoes off and sit here on the edge." He guided her to the raised deck that framed the pool. "I'll go get us some brandy."

He headed for the house.

9

Angela stepped out of her shoes, bent to remove her panty hose and then felt her way to the side of the pool. She sighed with relief as she eased her aching legs into the soothing heat. If only she knew Ricardo better, and could strip off all her clothes to submerge her whole, tired body.

The thought of sitting in the sensual pool with Ricardo sent tingles racing up her spine. Maybe later, they would—

"How does it feel?" His voice startled her.

"Wonderful." She kicked her feet to splash water in the air. The droplets sparkled as they reflected the faint traces of moonlight that filtered into the gazebo. The glasses clinked when Ricardo set them down near where she sat. His hand brushed her shoulder and then she felt him grasp her elbow.

"Stand up." He gave her a tug.

Angela drew her feet from the water and stood. She didn't need to see him to know he was very close. The lime scent that she'd breathed while they'd danced drifted about her. The heat of his body teased her into wanting to touch.

"Good, you still have your clothes on," he murmured.

Surprised, Angela asked as he pulled her into his embrace, "Why's that?"

"I wanted to take them off myself." He nuzzled at her neck.

"Ricardo, we're outside. In the yard."

"Shh, shh," he soothed. "I'll keep the lights off. No one'll see us."

The fear of being seen by neighbors wasn't her problem; it was Ricardo. Pings echoed on the redwood deck as he took the pins out of her chignon and let them drop. Her hair tumbled free.

Part of her held back, making her feel conservative and modest in front of this virtual stranger. And yet she longed to stand naked before the man and offer herself to him in the moonlight.

"There." Satisfaction toned his exclamation as he raked his fingers through her hair. "Now, for your jacket."

A tremor of desire shivered through her when he eased his warm hands under her collar to shrug the piece of clothing off her shoulders.

"Are you cold?" he asked, quick to respond to her every need.

"No, I—"

Before she could voice her doubts, his lips captured hers in a silencing kiss. Her heart raced and she grasped his arms to keep her balance. Caught up in the sensations coursing through her, she barely noticed that he'd undone the pearl buttons at the back of her blouse. The cool night air caressed her skin when he bared it.

"You're like silk." His breath fanned her cheeks as he mouthed kisses upon her face. His hands stroked down her back. Angela arched against his caress like a contented cat. The movement freed the front of her and Ricardo wasted no time in exploiting his advantage.

When his hands slid around her midriff to flatten on the soft belly of her stomach she sucked in a gasp of air.

"It's all right," he whispered as he stepped back, giving her breathing space. "We'll take this slow and easy."

Did she want "slow and easy" anymore? In fact, a strong urge clamored for her to rip off her clothes. She reached out for him, but he brushed her hand aside.

With acute awareness she watched him unbutton his shirt and peel off the fabric. It rustled to the floor and she strained her eyes in the dark to see him. A slight sheen, in the V shape of his torso, glistened in the silvery light.

"Hold me," she said, with desire in her voice.

He stepped close. Putting his hands on her waist he held her back. She reached up to grasp his arms but he pulled them away and placed her hands at her sides.

"Stand still," he murmured in a voice that soothed her tension. "We're not finished. I want you completely naked."

"And you?"

"Is that what you want?"

She reached up for him but he stepped aside, his laughter full of promise. "So impatient. Hold still and let me take care of you. We have the whole night to explore."

She clenched her fists and tried to control the trembling that shook her whole body. The brush of his knuckles against the curve of her breast startled her and she automatically jerked back.

"Easy now, *mi corazón*."

He undid the front clasp of her bra. Her swollen breasts ached for his touch. His fingers trembled as he removed the scanty lace, making Angela aware that he desired her as much as she did him.

He stepped back again and she listened to his movements. His belt buckle clattered loudly in the silence. She could only breathe in short gasps.

When he stood before her again she longed to throw herself into his arms but she waited, as he'd asked. Her heart hammered against her ribs. In seconds, the deft movements of his fingers sent her skirt rustling down to pool at her feet. Barely touching her, he slid off the last wisp of silk covering her body.

It seemed an eternity that they stood there. A breeze caught strands of her hair, feathering it across her skin, trailing tendrils that caught on Ricardo's shoulder.

He lifted her into his arms. The breeze had cooled his skin but it burned where it pressed against hers. She moaned, from deep in her throat—an animal sound that expressed her need.

Ricardo carried her down the steps and with tender care lowered her with him into the swirling hot water.

Clouds of steam, visible in the pale moonlight, rose around them. Angela tried to determine Ricardo's expression but could see only the dark silhouette of his head as he handed her a brandy snifter and raised his in the air.

"Here's to us." He clinked her glass in salute.

"To us," she repeated, her voice husky with emotion. What did that toast mean—*us as in lovers or us as in a relationship?* She wanted both.

The brandy warmed her. Water lapped at her breasts while jets of bubbles pounded on the muscles of her back.

"How does it feel?" he asked while he shifted close beside her.

"Like heaven," she told him, and closed her eyes in dreamy contentment. "All of the week's hassles have melted away."

"Did it make extra work for you with us taping in your room?"

"You were the biggest hassle," she teased.

"But I'm not melting away," he assured her. To emphasize his point he traced his finger along the waterline across her breasts.

Her initial lethargy from the heat disappeared when suddenly she felt the roughened skin on the tip of his finger begin to travel the peaks and valleys of her body. She held her breath until he finished.

His lazy pace disturbed her. What game was he playing—to torment her like this? She wanted him to continue, but he withdrew his hand and settled back in the pool.

"Ricardo." She couldn't help the groan of frustration. "Why did you stop?"

Laughter floated around her. Ricardo set down his snifter and reached for her. "Come here, sweetheart." He slid her onto his lap.

"What do you want?" he asked, tracing the shell of her ear with the tip of his tongue. "This?"

She slid her wet arms around his neck and pressed close against his chest. Turning, she planted tiny kisses on his eyelids, forehead and cheeks. "I want you to make love to me."

He shuddered beneath her. "I've wanted to hear you say that," he whispered.

"Is that what's been stopping you?"

"Who says I've stopped anything?" He teased his lips across hers. "Don't you like to experience the anticipation?"

She was enjoying that. But she wanted more. *Needed* more.

"You see if I touch you here—" he traced his finger along her neck "—or here—" it trailed down between her breasts and curved underneath "—it makes you want more."

"That's not all it does."

"But that is the joy of it."

The way his voice caressed sent shivers racing through her. She welcomed his touch and wanted him to make love to her, now, in the pool. Her seeming lack of inhibition surprised her. She struggled to sort out her feelings—desire mingled with love. *Love.* Did she *love* this man? It was too soon.

In a moment of doubt, she pushed herself away from Ricardo and sank to the bottom of the pool. Her hair tangled around her shoulders. Suddenly strong hands groped around her body until they settled about her waist. With a noisy splash Ricardo lifted her high in the air.

His laughter drifted into the night—laughter that was lusty and pleased. "So now you want to play," he exclaimed.

Angela braced her hands on his shoulders as she admitted to herself that maybe she did love this man. "I thought it took two for this game."

She wanted to learn everything she could. His muscles bulged from holding her up and they flexed when she began tracing their ridges.

"So, do you want to continue this play?" she asked after he shuddered.

"I want you."

"Tell me why?"

Slowly lowering her body, he turned to sit on the submerged bench. As he slid her down with him, his torso rubbed like electricity across her abdomen and her breasts. Angela gasped from the contact.

"There are many reasons I want you," he told her after settling her weight high on his waist. "You're beautiful and desirable, to begin with."

"Flimsy reason." She ran her fingers through his hair as she strove for light banter. It was impossible. The feel of his naked body beneath hers overwhelmed her. She wrapped her legs around his waist.

"Not enough?" he queried in mock surprise. "Let me see, could it be your body?"

"At this point, probably." She managed the wry humor. His body certainly governed *her* reactions.

"*¡Ay, querida!*" he moaned. "You underestimate me. There are other reasons, too."

"Such as?" Wouldn't he ever kiss her again? She ached for his caress. He had to be made of steel, because he didn't seem to react to the circles she traced on his chest.

"I like the way you care for others, the way you fight for your beliefs." He stopped her teasing caresses by grabbing her hands. The motion made waves and Angela shifted lower on his abdomen. If she slid another inch or two . . .

Angela wondered how much longer he could tease them both this way. Finally she'd had enough and silenced Ricardo with a kiss. When she pulled away she whispered into his mouth, "Let's get out of here."

Ricardo's reaction to her demand pleased her. In an almost-desperate haste he helped her to rise and step up from the pool. The night air cooled their overheated skin. Expecting him to turn on the light, Angela waited while he shuffled around to the far wall. In moments, he stood before her again and wrapped a huge fluffy towel around her shoulders.

Darkness surrounded them. Anxious now for what surely would follow, Angela's muscles knotted. She listened to his rustling in the dark and thought he must be dry by now. "Shall I get our clothes?" she asked. Surely they would go inside.

"Later," he said. "Lie down here."

Angela hesitated, unsure what he expected. Taking a deep breath, she bent to feel a padded mattress spread on the redwood decking. Surprise made her exclaim, "We're going to make love in here?"

"No. Not yet," he answered, his voice mysterious and seductive.

In the dim room she could see his outline as he stretched out on the mattress. Folds of fabric smoothed out beneath her fingers as she inched her way down beside Ricardo.

"A satin sheet?" she questioned. "Rather exotic for the pool isn't it?"

"It's like your skin." He curved his hand along the line of her hip and tucked her close beside him.

His body heat lured her to nuzzle close, but instead she touched the slick satin sheet—not with the tips of her fingers but with the full open palm of her hand. Its fine texture pleased her. She knew the feel of his skin would please her even more, but before she could reach out, he whispered.

"Lie on your stomach."

She hesitated, excitement creating havoc with her heart rate.

"I'm going to take good care of you."

With a gentle nudge he rolled her into a prone position. Shifting to his knees, he moved to kneel at her feet.
Angela's breath caught in her throat.

"Just relax and enjoy," he soothed as he lifted one
slender leg across his lap. "I'm going to begin at your
feet and cover all of you until I've rubbed away every
bit of stress I caused you this month."

A massage. His fingers began kneading her muscles.
A sound rumbled up from the depths of her being, a
purr of total contentment.

Ricardo listened to her moans of pleasure and felt a
strange peace assail him. He would never have guessed
that he could derive such pure satisfaction from pleas-
ing this woman.

Her tension eased with each firm prod of his fingers.
Once again he congratulated himself on his instinct to
leave the lights out and not rush her. He had felt her
apprehension several times. She needed, as he had
sensed, continuous cherishing and pampering to ensure her full-bodied desire. He wanted that for her.

"Is that better?" he asked as he worked out a stiff knot
in her back.

"Wonderful," she breathed. "You've hit places that
have been tied up for years."

"Years?" he exclaimed.

"I guess I let too many things upset me at work," she
admitted.

"What you need is a back rub every day when you
come home." The idea of being there to make sure she
got it appealed to him.

"I would think I'd died and gone to heaven," she
murmured.

He fell silent as he moved along her back, inching
closer with each sweep to the curves of her breasts. He

could feel the urge to slip his fingers underneath and enjoy the ripe fullness, but he refrained—for now.

At last he arrived at the tips of her fingers. He played with her reflexes, pressing nerve-sensitive spots until her slender fingers curled around his. To complete his ministrations on her arms, he nipped tiny kisses into the palm of her hand.

"Now for the other side," he announced as he rolled her onto her back.

"Hmm," she moaned. No inhibitions stiffened her body this time as he placed his hands on either side of her face.

Ricardo stretched out beside her, his body taut. *Madre mío.* He wanted her now. Now. This moment. She wouldn't hesitate to give her all to him—he knew it. But still he refrained.

"*Querida,*" he whispered before he feathered his lips on her closed eyelids, her temple and the sensitive curve of her neck.

"You're wonderful," she whispered. Her lazy voice traced sexy shivers along his spine.

"I want to kiss you all over." His heart hammered at the thought.

Suddenly she stiffened, only slightly but enough to alert Ricardo to her subtle uneasiness. *Not yet,* he decided. "For breakfast," he promised her.

Ricardo shifted to his knees to massage her. Carefully he traced over her breasts, enjoying their fullness. He marveled at the symmetry of her hips and how they framed the pliant muscles of her stomach. His hands tracked across her thighs as he fought the temptation to explore the promised place waiting for him.

By the time he reached her toes, every nerve was stretched taut with overtaxed restraint. Never had he pressured himself to this point, and he wondered if he had overestimated his willpower.

Not a word had been spoken during these last long minutes. His whole body had been focused on the silky feel of her skin, and the curves beneath his fingers had invited thoughts that constricted his throat.

In an effort to gain some measure of control Ricardo rocked back on his heels. He took deep breaths of the steamy air that was heavy with the scent of flowers— and of Angela.

Careful not to disturb her, he stretched out on the satin sheet. Warmth radiated from her body as it re-flected the moonlight. With fingers that trembled, he reached out to touch her breast.

"Umm," she moaned, sending shivers through his body. "Hold me, Ricardo."

That was it. There would be no more temptation. He was ready to make her his.

"Come on, darling," he whispered into the cloud of silvery hair that billowed around her. "Let's go to bed."

He lifted her nude body into his arms and carried her across the lawn and into the house. He passed through the back entryway, down the hall and into the master bedroom where he placed her on his bed. His bedside lamp bathed her in a soft glow. At last he could admire her to his heart's content.

Angela's eyes adjusted to the lamplight, and a slow heat began to build as she admired Ricardo's muscular physique.

Surely he couldn't wait any longer—not as aroused as he was. "Are you going to love me now?"

"Yes, *querida*. We are going to love each other."

Before joining her, he quickly took care of protec-tion. He climbed onto the bed, his weight shifting her toward him. Leaning on one elbow, he reclined on his side and smiled.

"Are you ready now?" she asked as she lifted her arms to wrap them around his shoulders.

"More than ready. And you?"

She nodded and began to speak but her words died on her lips when he gently pushed her legs apart. He slid his hand up her thighs and moved his fingers into intimate territory.

He smothered her gasp with his kiss and he nudged her back down again, spreading her legs. He teased and caressed her. Her desire became uncontrollable whenever his fingers probed the nub of her sex.

Angela reciprocated the intimate caresses that made her body tingle. She could feel the same response in Ricardo. His muscles tensed wherever she touched, rippling and flexing in readiness. How it pleased her to know she could do that to him.

She pulled him to her. He resisted, forcing her hands to her side and placing her knees wide apart.

"Not yet." He panted.

"Yes. Now." The sweet torture was making her wild. Suddenly she couldn't take any more. "Now, Ricardo. Now. I want you deep inside me. All of you."

She struggled free and wrapped her arms around his neck and pulled his mouth to hers, kissing him urgently.

He groaned and rolled between her legs. *At last*. She wrapped her limbs around his waist and writhed.

Ricardo was poised at the entrance. Angela froze, afraid he'd tease her again. "Fill me, Ricardo."

"Is this what you want?"

"Yes," she begged, tossing her head back and forth while arching toward him.

Ricardo entered her. Angela moaned with pleasure, loving the hard feel of him.

"My sweet angel," Ricardo murmured. And then he started to thrust.

Her release was the most intense, pleasurable one she'd ever experienced. Ricardo's climax followed hers. Then he collapsed over her. For several minutes neither one of them moved as they caught their breath and reveled in the sensations they'd felt.

"That was perfect," Ricardo whispered as he rolled onto his back and placed her head on his shoulder.

Angela slid her leg over his and molded her curves against him. Moonlight filtered across their bodies after Ricardo turned off the light. Loving Ricardo had been so good. So right. But morning was only hours away.

SUNLIGHT FILTERED through the half-closed mini-blinds, creating stripes across the carpet. Angela blinked several times to adjust her vision to the unfamiliar sight. She rolled over onto her back and stretched with lazy pleasure.

"Slept well?" His deep voice sent waves of longing through her. Memories of the night flooded her.

She cast a sleepy glance in his direction. A seductive smile etched across his face. He posed on one elbow so that his weight shifted to his side, leaving one hand free to reach for her. He did so with unsteady fingers and stroked her breasts.

She searched his face for his intentions. She saw passion, but more important, she saw caring.

"Good morning," she murmured.

"Did I wake you?"

She shook her head, glad she was awake and not missing another moment of this.

"Did you sleep well?"

"How could I not after last night . . . ?" Her voice trailed off as vivid memories brought with them a feeling of vulnerability.

"Was it special for you?"

Incredibly so, but she didn't say it. She merely nodded. "And you?" she asked, wanting confirmation.

He started to reach for her but hesitated. Obviously he had his own vulnerabilities. Since he hadn't rushed her into making love, she wouldn't force words of commitment from him.

Reaching across the space between them, she traced her fingers down his jaw, to the skin of his neck and finally to his chest.

"You were . . ." He started to speak, but she silenced him with the tips of her fingers.

Smiling with mischievous intent, she returned to explore the planes of his chest. The hard ridges pleased her and she feathered her fingers across them, aware of the effect she had on his control. He tensed and she could almost hear the drumming beats of his heart—or were they her own?

He reached out, sure and steady this time, and pulled a lock of hair from behind her. Holding the ends he brushed them across the hardened peaks of her breasts in a circular motion. Angela's muscles ached and again the yearning to have him inside her consumed her.

But not like last night. She didn't have the patience for the slow, tormenting pace he had set then. Giving a mighty shove, she toppled him onto his back and followed with quick action. She braced her elbows on his chest, her hair forming a curtain of intimacy, and smiled down at him.

"You took care of me last night," she told him. "Now I'll take care of you this morning."

With promise in her eyes, she bent to his responsive mouth.

Gasping for breath, he spoke when she lifted her head. "I think I'm going to like this."

She smiled, letting him see the love she felt for him. "Now, it's my turn . . . to lead."

"Why, you . . ." He laughed and shifted sideways, the movement rolling her onto her back. "You've been holding out on me."

"No." Her expression grew serious. "You were right. I needed the time to go slow last night."

"And now?" He searched deep into her eyes.

"Now it's my turn, as you recall."

She cast him a mischievous glance. In one sweeping tangle of sheets and bodies, she rolled him on his back and straddled his waist.

Grabbing his wrists, she pinned his arms beside his head. They both knew he could easily break free of his imprisonment, but they also both knew he wouldn't. Angela could see that he was thoroughly enjoying the nips on his neck and shoulder, and the way her breasts brushed across his chest when she leaned down.

Holding him didn't take effort, but containing herself did. She forced deep breaths to calm her body's insistence that she end the play. Arching her back she let her chest expand with each breath, delighting in the way his eyes widened in time to her movements.

He shifted as if to take over but she tightened her knees against his sides. He stilled but she saw the cost of his effort. Muscles bunched beneath his olive skin.

Love Lessons 139

She could feel his flex press against her sensitive inner thighs.

She moaned, wondering how long she could prolong the teasing.

As if sensing her weakening, Ricardo spoke, his voice husky and low: "Now, *mi Angelita*. Have mercy."

She shook her head, sending wisps of hair feathering across his stomach. His flat muscles hardened and Angela smiled, pleased with herself.

Finally she gave in, releasing his wrists.

Ricardo reached toward the nightstand. She pressed him back to the bed and leaned over him.

"Let me do it," she whispered.

Gently she sheathed him with protection and then just as gently sheathed him with her body.

From that moment on, her only thought was to give him her all until the final, delicious release.

10

BRIGHT SUNLIGHT reflected off the water in the pool. Angela donned her sunglasses to cut the glare before she sat down at the wrought-iron table.

"Are you hungry, *querida*?" Ricardo asked before he nipped lightly at her neck.

"We did skip breakfast," she reminded him while pouring fresh-squeezed orange juice into glasses.

"I recall having a great breakfast."

Angela flushed—more from the memories of his ardor than from embarrassment. Avoiding his knowing glance, she selected several pieces of fresh fruit, some slices of cheese and a hunk of French bread. Remembering the exquisite joys they had shared made her head spin.

"Do you want some melon?"

He took the plate of honeydew and served them both a slice. Angela watched him, knowing her feelings of love were obvious, but she sensed he didn't mind.

"What do you want to do for the rest of the day?" he asked.

"Whatever." She shrugged. As long as she spent it with him, it didn't matter to her what they did.

"It'll be hard to top the morning." He winked and then reached over to plop a succulent strawberry into her mouth. "But we'll try."

While the sweet juices of the strawberry satisfied her hunger, his sensual reminder filled her with renewed longing. She couldn't stop the tide of sensations that flooded her every time she thought about the past few hours. From the expression that crossed his face, she guessed he felt the same.

"We could relax by the pool," she suggested, while picturing images of where that could lead.

"I have one errand I need to make." He tore a piece of flaky crust and placed it in his mouth.

"We could stop by your place on the way back and pick up some clothes," he suggested before he leaned forward to trace his finger down the line of her collar. "But on the other hand, I like the way you're dressed now."

Her sharp intake of breath was the only sound as his finger trailed to her cleavage. Angela glanced down to see that his robe she had borrowed lay open, almost to her navel. She closed the black silk in spite of being overly warm.

"I think we'd better make that stop." She cast him a rueful grin. "Besides, I'll need my swimsuit."

Actually, she didn't mind wearing his robe. Designed to fall just below his hips, it covered her almost to her knees. Of course, the rolled-up sleeves were awkward but the scents of Ricardo that enveloped her more than made up for the inconvenience.

"Bring something in case we decide to go out tonight." He reached across the table with another strawberry.

She accepted the offering, not resisting the time he took to trace her bottom lip. "And tomorrow?" she murmured lazily.

"Hmm." He seemed distracted as he stared at her mouth. "We could take a drive to the desert. The cacti are in bloom."

Purposely she licked her lips with the tip of her tongue. His eyes dilated just as she hoped they would. "We could stop by my folks,'" she suggested.

Where had that invitation slipped out from? Was she ready for him to meet her family?

"Ah...just teasing." She backtracked. "You wouldn't want to go there."

In dismay, she watched his eyes narrow as he studied her quick reversal. She cursed her inability to hide her reactions from this man. He probably wouldn't have batted an eye at her suggestion, but now, because of her discomfort, he was closely scrutinizing her.

"Why not?" The tone of his voice sounded casual, but she saw the rigidity of his body.

"It's just a family get-together." She shrugged and prayed he wouldn't pursue it further. "My two brothers bring their wives and kids every Sunday to my parents' home in Scottsdale."

Which was the exact reason she never brought her dates. Overprotective and assertive, her brothers intimidated the unsuspecting males with their third degree. They had been unmerciful at times, and she had finally just stopped bringing her dates home. Who knew what they would think of Ricardo? But then, maybe that was why the invitation had slipped out: She had a feeling Ricardo could hold his own with her older siblings.

"I don't mind going." Ricardo sipped his coffee and watched her over the rim of the cup, his expression guarded. "If they're expecting you, we can stop by. Besides, I like family gatherings."

Eager to change the subject, Angela took advantage of the cue. "Do you have family in Phoenix?"

"They're all in Los Angeles. Four brothers and two sisters." His eyes lit with genuine warmth as he thought of them. "They all converge on *mi mamá* every Sunday, too. So you see—a family get-together would be no *problema*."

"I guess I really don't want to go, now that I think about it. Let's just spend the time together."

"Is it because of me you changed your mind about going to see your family?"

"What are you talking about?"

"Are you ashamed for them to know you are intimate with me?"

Angela stared, disbelief mingling with sudden anger. "Ricardo, after all we've been through, you have the nerve to accuse me of that?"

"You invited me to your parents' home and then immediately changed your mind."

"Here we go again. That deep-seated problem of self-esteem. When does it stop? How does it end?" Angela stood and swung around, afraid that if she continued to look at him she'd want to pound him with her fists. She took a shaky breath and tried to control the quiver in her voice. "How could you make love to me? Do you feel that way about me?"

Ricardo was behind her in seconds, grasping her shoulders and pulling her around. "Hey, what's all this? I was teasing you. All of a sudden you fly off the handle. What're you talking about?"

Now she felt rather foolish. "It's not something to tease about. I thought I'd hurt your feelings."

"Me? You're looking at a man with tough skin. It's been a long time since anyone's hurt me." He tucked her hair behind her ear and then trailed his fingers along her neck. "You, though, *querida*, could be the one to do that. I'm beginning to care a lot about you."

Her pulse quickened. Caring preceded love. "I care for you, too. And I wouldn't do anything to hurt you."

"No, you're too sensitive for that. So what's the verdict, anyway? We were discussing a visit to your parents' tomorrow. Is it a go or not?"

"I'd like you to meet them. But I'll warn you—I don't usually take men to visit."

"Hmm." He rocked back on his heels and grinned. "Does this prove how special I am?"

"Maybe."

He curved his fingers around her neck and pulled her to him. His kiss was sensual and demanding, leaving her breathless and hungry for more.

"I'm not a coward."

Definitely not. She smiled. Her brothers were going to meet their match in Ricardo.

"My parents are going to think this is serious."

"Isn't it?"

Was he still teasing? Before she could ask, he kissed her again. Long and hard.

When their kiss ended he held her in his arms and studied her face. "I can't decide if I like you better like this, or full of fire over one of your causes."

She noticed the glints of mischief in his eyes.

"So, tell me," he continued. "Am I special?"

"Shall I list all the ways? Like you did last night for me?"

"Would you have enough time?"

She knew just what he needed. She poked him in the chest and took a step forward. "Not enough time, huh?"

He backed up. She moved forward.

"You think the list is so long?" she quipped. "Don't get the idea I think you're a saint."

"Surely I must be close." He chuckled, caught up in her good humor.

"You're close, all right." To the edge of the pool, she meant. "After all, you're dedicated to your causes, ambitious, caring, sympathetic." She smiled innocently and poked him one last time. "You're also going to get wet."

His arms flailed as he tried to regain his balance before landing with a splash in the pool. He came up sputtering and shaking the wet hair from his face.

"You fox!" He glared when she laughed. "I'll show you what we do in my culture with such clever ones."

The threat was barely spoken before he was scrambling out of the pool and after Angela. With a screech of mock alarm, she raced into the house. Ricardo reached her before she could shut the door.

He chased her down the hall and into the bedroom, where he finally grabbed hold of the trailing belt of his robe.

Angela didn't struggle too hard when he directed her into the bathroom and into his arms. "You're wet and cold."

"Now, why is that?"

"Really. You shouldn't go swimming with your clothes on."

He nuzzled her neck. Angela flinched when he opened the robe and pressed her bare body against his wet one.

"I take it all back. You aren't even close to being wonderful. You're mean and a bully."

She attempted to escape and ended up completely naked as he continued to hold on to the robe. His smile wavered slightly as he took in the sight of her. The teasing went out of his expression, to be replaced by lust.

She backed up until she bumped into the shower door where she paused, assessing her options. Ricardo blocked the exit. Her heart raced as she anticipated the sweet revenge he had in store for her.

"Now we'll see what happens to sexy ladies who have the nerve to push innocent men into pools."

"Innocent?" She watched, wide-eyed and curious as he shed his still-dripping clothes. "That's one trait I never said you had."

He started toward her. Stalking. Ready. "But I have other traits you like, no?"

Her gaze lowered to just below his waist. "Definitely," she managed to say.

He wrapped his arms around her and held her against his hard body. This time he wasn't cold. His skin burned when he cupped her behind and lifted her for a closer fit.

Her toes barely touched the tile as she wrapped her arms around his neck. She forgot about their argument. He carried her into the shower.

Cold water splashed on her head and down her back. Angela screamed.

He held her tightly, his body vibrating with laughter. "Vengeful, my love. That's another trait that maybe you didn't know about."

My love. Those two words drowned out the rest of what he'd said. The water didn't even feel cold. The only sensations were a deep longing for those two simple words to have full meaning. *Love.* She wanted his love.

Heedless of the cold spray, she drew his head down to hers and kissed him hard. At first he maintained his playful mood but he soon grew serious as her demand became more insistent.

"Love me," she whispered between kisses. "Take me now."

He grinned. "This revenge is turning into a reward."

"You said I was clever." She shifted so he could adjust the temperature of the water. The cascade turned warm to match the heat she was feeling.

"I don't know if you deserve this."

"Oh? We could leave, then." She turned toward the door but his arms wrapped around her and he kept her against him. Exactly where she wanted to be.

"You're not escaping now."

The water made it easier to slide close to his body, and the friction aroused both of them. He lifted her easily. She wrapped her legs around his waist and moaned when he pulled her against his erection.

"If this is your kind of revenge, I'm going to think of all kinds of ways to torment you."

"Brazen hussy." He traced his hand down her spine and curved his fingers between the cleft of her rear. "I suppose you're one of those women who's impossible to satisfy."

"Could be. I've never felt this way before. I guess we'll have to find out."

"Like in school?"

"By all means let's be scientific."

"We need to explore." He ran his fingers down her back and curved underneath to tease the sensitive skin.

"Don't do that," she gasped.

"Do what? This?" He inched farther. "Or this?" His fingers toyed with intimate places.

"Science was never so good." She arched while at the same time tightening her legs around him.

Talking ceased as his exploration grew more intense. Her fingers dug into his shoulders. Water splashed crazily over them, but Angela hardly noticed. She wanted to open her eyes and watch the expression of passion on Ricardo's face, but her eyelids were too heavy.

"Are you ready?"

"Yes. Now," she begged.

"It's too soon. I want this to last forever."

Carefully he eased her off him and lowered her to her feet. The shower stall seemed to spin crazily as she clung for support. He held her around the waist with one arm while his other hand caressed her.

"Haven't you had enough revenge? This is torture." She slid her arms from his shoulders and braced herself against the wall, letting the ceramic tiles cool her down.

"But I told you. Revenge is so sweet." He took the soap and began sudsing bubbles all over her body. "Besides, we need to bathe if we're going out."

"You're right." She pretended to acquiesce but as soon as he leaned forward to soap her back, she reached for him.

He paused, closing his eyes to savor the pleasure. "You keep that up and you aren't going to get this soap . . ."

She applied gentle pressure, cutting off his words. "The bubbles make you so slick and smooth," she murmured into his mouth before kissing him.

He gasped for breath when she'd finished the kiss. "You're playing with fire. I'm going . . ."

Again she caressed him and he groaned. She smiled, liking how easily she could control him. "What were you saying about fire? We're underwater here. Surely—"

This time he cut off her conversation by pressing his lips over hers. In a slow tortuous descent he traced his fingers down her throat to cup each breast. With his thumb he scored the sensitive tips until she twisted away from his hands so she could crush against him.

"Two can play this game," he told her.

"You're asking for it."

"I know. I want you."

Angela stood on her toes, wanting him to take her. Now.

Slowly he backed out of her embrace and rinsed the soap off their bodies, watching water trickle over and down her curves. He followed several rivulets with his tongue, but when he reached her waist, she grabbed his head between her hands and drew it up to hers.

"No more playing, Ricardo." She kissed him, entwining her arms across his shoulders. Hoisting herself up, she again wrapped her legs around his waist. "Finish it this time."

His laughter was throaty as he did her bidding and entered her. She arched her body as he thrust deeply.

They reached the climactic finish together. Angela screamed, Ricardo groaned—their sounds combining pleasure and release.

She lowered her legs to the rough flooring but her muscles were too slack to stand on. Ricardo braced her against him, giving her time to regain her balance.

"Did I deserve an *A* on that one, *maestra?*" he asked, his breath still coming in gasps.

She nodded, enjoying the joke for a minute. But then she grew serious. "You can have all the revenge you want."

"That good, huh?" he quipped, though his smile disappeared as he responded to the intensity of her gaze.

"Yes, that good." She reached up and framed his face in her hands. She wanted to say *I love you*.

"You're pretty special, yourself."

His expression assured her that he meant it. She couldn't ask for more. Not yet.

Not sure she could handle any more intimacy without telling him of her love, Angela backed away from his body and let the water wash over her.

"I'm special, all right. It's not every day you can make love with a prune."

Her skin was beginning to wrinkle.

"Not a prune. More like a wet fish."

"Wet fish? Are you looking for more trouble?"

They continued to banter while they dressed. Their good spirits held throughout the afternoon. Angela forgot about school and being a teacher as Ricardo fulfilled his promise and proceeded to give her a relaxing weekend.

The trip to her apartment and his errand didn't take long. After they took a leisurely tour through the nearby Heard Museum, they spent the rest of the afternoon walking along the paths of Encanto Park.

A small art fair was set up along the edge of the park and Angela persuaded Ricardo to stop for a few minutes to watch an artist make flowers out of blown glass.

"Isn't it just fascinating to watch how easily they form such delicate shapes?"

When he didn't answer, she glanced at him and caught his contemplative stare. "There are other things more fascinating to watch."

Angela grinned and noticed the artist was smiling also. They left the fair and stopped to feed the ducks before they continued their walk along the twisting paths of the park. Ricardo let her set the pace for the day and Angela kept it relaxed.

He'd planned to take her to dinner at a nearby restaurant but she didn't really care to be in a crowd. She wanted Ricardo all to herself—at his home where she could reach out and touch or steal a kiss.

They barbecued on the patio and sat by the side of the pool, talking late into the evening. They delved into their private lives. The more Angela talked with Ricardo, the stronger her love grew. She was glad he was meeting her family. This was turning out to be very serious, indeed.

RICARDO DOWNSHIFTED as he approached the curve. The Ferrari cornered easily on the road that wound through Papago Park toward Scottsdale. It was a beautiful day. Just right for a Sunday drive. But he couldn't shake his growing uneasiness.

They'd left much later than the time they'd decided on. But he was sure Angela didn't mind that. She seemed to thrive on their lovemaking as much as he did.

He glanced over at her. The breeze tossed her hair, much the same way it mussed when they were in bed. He got hard just thinking about it.

As he drove, he reflected on the experience of these past hours. He'd known Angela was going to be special. He just hadn't realized how much.

Every time they made love it was as if she took another brick out of the wall around his inner self. He would have guessed that the exposure would be threatening. Yet apprehension wasn't what he was feeling— but instead, an amazing feeling of trust and openness.

At least he'd felt secure until now. With each mile that brought them closer to her parents' home, he grew more tense and guarded. Angela's own anxiety only heightened his. He cast another glance at her. Now she was clenching her fists tightly in her lap.

"Okay. Out with it," he said. "You're getting more tense with each passing minute. Do you want to turn around and go back?" The idea seemed more and more appealing.

"I *am* nervous. What I said yesterday about not wanting you to meet my family—it's true. But it's not what you think."

"I'm listening."

"It's my brothers. They're extremely protective. They're going to give you the third degree when I bring you home."

"Your brothers?" He gripped the leather-covered steering wheel to curve around the last corner before the downhill stretch into Scottsdale. "What exactly are they going to be concerned about?"

"Me. They're going to want to know everything about you, if your intentions toward me are honest...."

"Like in marriage?" His chest constricted. He wasn't ready for that yet. Or was he?

"No. Not that bad. But you see, I was burned once. Badly. It was actually due to my own poor judgment. But they're going to make sure you know they won't allow it to happen again."

"They're intimidating? Is that what you're warning me about?" What he really wanted to ask was who had hurt her. Then again, maybe it was just as well he didn't know. It could be he had something in common with her brothers.

"'Intimidating' is expressing it mildly. They're big guys and they play rough. Like I mentioned earlier, I don't usually bring dates home."

"Does this mean you're getting revenge for this morning and are throwing me to the lions?"

The smile she flashed him chased away his doubts. "I think you can handle them. It'll serve them right to meet someone who isn't intimidated."

"Sounds like a challenge." He grinned. "You know I love challenges."

Angela laughed. "Don't say I didn't warn you." She flung her hand in a gesture of concession.

Ricardo grasped her fingers and pulled them into his lap. "Look. I've been in a lot of tough spots. I always land on my feet."

This kind of trouble he could handle. He knew exactly where her brothers were coming from. "Remember. I have sisters. Me and my brothers had quite a few tricks of our own."

"Are your sisters younger than you?"

"One is. They're both married now, so we've been able to relax."

"That's encouraging. I'd hate to think I was going to have to put up with this forever."

IT DIDN'T TAKE MORE than a few minutes at her parents' home for Ricardo to realize Angela's anxiety had been well-founded. Her brothers were determined to size him up.

Outwardly they were polite, but the subtle probing never ended. Ricardo was comfortable with that. After all, it was what he did on the job. Fielding verbal challenges was a piece of cake for him.

Since they were making no progress in intimidating him verbally, Howard and Dave challenged him to join a family volleyball game, obviously planning to show him up in a so-called sporting match.

Physically they were well matched. Ricardo was as tall, lean and fit as her brothers. But there were two of them. This posed a real problem, as he was now discovering.

"Your serve, Angela." Her older brother Howard tossed her the wet volleyball.

Ricardo crouched in the four feet of water where the net stretched across the game-style swimming pool. The depth didn't vary as in most pools. It was built for swimming laps and playing volleyball, so he wouldn't have to worry about getting into deep water.

Literally, anyway. Figuratively, he just might be in over his head. Howard and Dave grinned at him from the opposite side of the net. Not friendly smiles but feral grins. They were clearly athletes primed for attack. Beside them, their wives appeared to play the game but mainly tried to stay out of the way.

On his side, Angela did what she could. So did her mother and father. But the real game was between Howard, Dave and Ricardo.

Angela served the ball. Dave's wife sent it to Howard. Ricardo tensed, knowing the ball would go to Dave next for a front-net spike. Ricardo moved to the net and jumped the same time Dave did, and blocked the ball.

"Way to go!" Angela cheered.

He turned to give her a smile of triumph, but not before seeing the glance exchanged between Howard and Dave. *Good.* He had them worried.

"I'll cover you here," Angela's father assured him.

It was a small victory. Her father wasn't offering full support yet. He played but he didn't interfere with his sons' challenge. Ricardo knew the man was holding back and taking Ricardo's measure. That was cool. At least he wasn't blocking progress.

Angela scored two more points before she lost her serve. It was Dave's turn now. Ricardo groaned. Angela's brother had a fast and mean serve. It came right at him. He tipped it but Angela missed.

"Sorry."

"Next time."

The ball whizzed at him again. He got it over the net but it was high. A perfect setup for Howard, who took advantage and spiked it at Ricardo. Having barely recovered from the first hit, he missed.

"Tough break," Angela's father sympathized.

Ricardo knew better. It wasn't chance. Howard and Dave were out to kill. From the way Angela's father observed his reaction, he knew this was the final showdown.

Angela must have sensed it, too. "Stop picking on Ricardo!" she hollered across the net. "We're in this game, too. You can hit the ball to us."

Howard and Dave held up their hands in innocence but Ricardo was no fool. He bunched his muscles for the next attack. The women moved to the side of the pool. The ball came fast and hard. He jumped higher than the net, water splashing from his body, and smashed the ball directly between Howard and Dave.

A loud guffaw greeted him as he broke through the water on his recovery. Angela's father came toward him and slapped him on the back.

"Good show, son. My boys deserve this."

Ricardo glanced through the net, expecting to see a pair of disgruntled players. But the two men were laughing. Ricardo let out his breath. He'd made it. Passed the mark.

The game continued, but at a relaxed pace. Everyone had a chance to join in, now that he'd been tested. Howard and Dave's team wound up winning the game but Ricardo didn't worry about that. He'd won acceptance.

LATER THAT EVENING, after he'd parked his car in the visitors' lot at Angela's apartment complex, she mentioned the game.

"You didn't get upset when my brothers ganged up on you."

"That's what they wanted me to do."

"I know. You men play such ridiculous games. What did it prove, anyway? I mean, what if you couldn't play volleyball? Am I supposed to not be interested in you?"

"It wasn't how good I was, but how I played. I didn't let them intimidate me and I played fair."

"You were a good sport. I was ready to bash their heads in."

Ricardo laughed. He wouldn't treat Angela with dishonesty or unfairness. Her brothers would bash in *his* head for that. They'd also established his integrity. Her father had understood, as well.

"I enjoyed your family. They were a lot of fun." Once the game had ended, they all had treated him as if he belonged. Ricardo appreciated that. "I miss my family. They're a lot like yours. Lots of teasing. Lots of laughs."

"And how about the food? I'm stuffed." She shifted as if in pain.

He empathized. "I haven't eaten like that since the last time I visited *mi mamá*. Your mom's a good cook. Do you take after her?"

"Don't get your hopes up. If it doesn't cook in five minutes, I don't eat it."

Ricardo began gathering her things before he got out of the car. "How do you manage that?"

"The meat goes on the gas grill. The potato in the microwave and then a vegetable or salad. Simple and quick. I promise it's nutritious and delicious." She stepped out as he opened the door for her. "Are you coming in?"

Ricardo hesitated, wanting to follow her inside and spend another night. But he felt the need for breathing space and he suspected Angela did, too, especially when she didn't argue his decision to go home.

"You're probably right." She stopped at her door and turned to him. "It's Sunday night. Tomorrow's work and I have a million things to do."

"I don't want the weekend to end." And he didn't. In some ways it seemed as if they'd been together forever. It felt right, natural. Maybe that feeling made him a little nervous.

Angela unlocked her door and took her bag from him. After setting it on the floor she turned and smiled. "Thanks for everything."

He curled his hand around the back of her neck, his thumb stroking the soft skin. Her windblown hair curled around his fingers. Suntan lotion mingled with her scent and tantalized her senses. Maybe he would stay.

"Are you relaxed now? All the work-week stress forgotten?"

"Definitely." She stood on tiptoe and brushed her lips across his. "Will I see you this week?"

He frowned, not liking to think about his schedule. "I'm going to the board meeting on Tuesday. Are you?"

She nodded.

"By then I'll know what's lined up for work." He brushed her lips this time. "Keep the weekend open. We'll figure something out."

It wasn't like him to commit so far in advance, especially in a relationship as new as this one. But suddenly he wanted the assurance that Angela would be there.

When she smiled, he pulled her against him and kissed her. His arms wrapped around her as if it was where they belonged. She felt so good. Too good. He pulled away.

"If we keep this up any longer, I'm going to change my mind."

The blue of her eyes had deepened in color and her lids looked heavy, as if hiding the flare of desire. He groaned and kissed her again, trying to ignore the invitation in her glance.

Reluctantly he let her go. "Sweet dreams, *querida*."

She looked about to say something but quickly stepped away. Ricardo hesitated and then, with a wave, headed down the path to the parking lot.

As he approached the black sports car he stretched his aching muscles. *¡Caramba!* It had been some day. What he needed was a soak in the Jacuzzi. But he had a feeling it wouldn't help him. There were too many memories of Angela, naked in the pool, delightful in the shower, warm and willing in his bed. He had a feeling those memories were going to occupy his mind for many hours to come.

ANGELA SHUT THE DOOR after watching Ricardo disappear from sight around the corner. In a daze she put away her things. She hated to see Ricardo leave but she also felt relieved to have time to herself.

She couldn't believe she'd almost told him she loved him. When he'd kissed her goodbye, the words had seemed so right. How could she feel so strongly after just one weekend together? He couldn't possibly feel the same way. If she'd said the words, he probably would have turned tail and run as far away as he could get.

You didn't say them, so relax, she chided herself. But while she switched on the stereo and began to tackle her chores, images floated in and out of her head. The picture of her in Ricardo's arms was too vivid and it was too easy to imagine her saying, "I love you."

A couple of hours later, Angela sat on her couch, droopy eyed and tired. Her laundry was done, her hair washed and the apartment vacuumed. The idyllic hours spent with Ricardo seemed eons away.

Able to relax at last, she allowed herself the pleasure of relishing her memories of the weekend. It pleased her immensely that Ricardo had made a hit with her family. But then she'd suspected he would. But more important than that were *her* feelings.

They weren't hard to define. All she had to do was think about the way he held her when they danced. How his fingers felt massaging her body. The firm nip of his lips as he kissed her everywhere. *Hmm. Wonderful. Heavenly. Divine.*

The phone rang, jarring her out of her dreams. Her muscles, stiff from all the "unusual" activity of the weekend, protested when she struggled to rise.

"Hello." She hoped it was Ricardo, missing her already.

Mrs. Edwards spoke into the phone.

Angela groaned and slumped onto the couch. Reality had returned too soon.

"Sorry to bother you on a Sunday night," her principal apologized. "But I tried to get through to you all weekend."

"It's all right. I was still up. What can I do for you?"

"I need to see you first thing in the morning. Looks like the board is considering a staff reduction. You might be on the list to be laid off."

11

WHEN ANGELA ARRIVED at school the next morning she was a nervous wreck. The strain of her sleepless night showed in the dark shadows under her eyes. Irritable before the day even started, Angela entered Mrs. Edwards's office.

"Sit here, Angela." The principal gestured toward a chair. "Before you get all upset, keep in mind the decision hasn't been made yet to enforce the R.I.F."

A reduction in force. "When will they know?"

"They're waiting for confirmation of government funds. If they come through, we can keep our staff. If not . . ."

Angela knew what that meant. "But why me? I've been here five years. Surely I'm high on the seniority list."

"True. Your name's just below the cutoff point. If enough people above you retire or resign, it could put you over."

This couldn't be happening. Not after all these years! She didn't think she could stand to lose her job a second time. What would she say to her family? Her last layoff had been hard on them. But it had been associated with a scandal, making it an emotional strain as well as a financial one. The R.I.F. would be determined by lack of seniority. But still, she'd have to ask for financial support until she landed another job. Who knew when or where that would be?

"Is there anything I can do about this?"

"Just wait. We aren't announcing it officially until we know for sure. No sense getting the parents in an uproar."

Somehow she couldn't work up sympathy for the community. Not with her world falling around her. She'd just hurdled the attack from Ricardo about the whole-language program. Now she had to face this. Angela pressed on her stomach, willing it to settle down.

"I'm notifying everyone here that's affected. We'll operate on the assumption you're going to be offered a contract for next year. But, just in case . . ."

As the principal's voice droned on, Angela barely registered what she said. She was agitated and anxious and remained so for the rest of the day. She'd hoped that the hustle and bustle of her class might help her forget. At least it would keep her too occupied to think about all the possibilities.

To her dismay, being in the classroom had had the opposite effect. The day had turned into a disaster. She was relieved when the bell had rung and her students had finally gone home.

"What are you moping around about?" Maria startled her.

Resting her head on her arms, Angela abruptly sat up at her desk and peered at Maria. She could barely manage a weak smile.

"Did the kids wear you out today or do you miss that gorgeous hunk of manhood?" Maria teased.

Feeling defensive and definitely grumpy, Angela stood up. The silk folds of her purple dress slid back in place across her slender figure.

"Come on, I'll buy you a cola." Angela grabbed her purse and strode to the door. Maybe conversation with Maria would distract her. She didn't think she could cope with discussing the possible layoff. She needed time to sort her feelings.

"You aren't getting away with this," Maria informed Angela as they stretched their legs across the extra chairs of the empty teachers' lounge. "Something's got you down. You know it helps to talk about it."

"I suppose you're right. Have you heard about the R.I.F.?"

"At lunch. You aren't on it, are you?"

"You hit the nail on the head."

Maria straightened, almost sending her can of soda across the room. "You're kidding! But you've been in the district for . . ."

"I know. I know. Five years. That fact has been repeating itself in my brain all day. I just can't believe it."

For several minutes they discussed the issue, but both knew it was pointless. There was nothing anyone could do.

"Have you told Ricardo?"

"No. And I don't intend to."

"But why? He still has influence on the board. Maybe he can speak on your behalf."

Angela rolled her eyes skyward. Hadn't her friend figured out that asking Ricardo for help would be the last thing she'd do? "I can just see it. History repeating itself. All I need is for some teacher to accuse me of having an affair with Ricardo to secure my position at school."

"An affair?" Maria's eyebrows rose.

Angela cringed. She'd let that detail slip out.

"What happened this weekend that I don't know about?"

Normally, Angela would have been more reticent, but she was really down today. Besides, Maria was her best friend. She'd find out sooner or later.

"I love him."

Now she had said the words, her mind was cleared of the stress of the day and left with the sweet promise of love.

Maria, too, forgot about the R.I.F. "That's wonderful! How does he feel? How can you be so sad?" A million questions popped out of Maria's mouth before Angela could answer a single one.

Heaving a wistful sigh, Angela shushed her friend and told her what had happened. Not the intimate details, but Maria wasn't dense; Angela could tell by Maria's sly grin that her friend had filled in her own version of the facts.

"If he cares for you, then you must figure he's going to want to help you out."

Vigorously she shook her head. "If he does, that will be the end for us. I can't risk it."

The thought saddened her. She'd just found love. Would she lose it so soon?

"I think you should talk this over with him," said Maria. "You should clarify your position for yourself as well as for your job."

"You're right," Angela conceded reluctantly. Her friend's logic did make sense. "I'll think about it."

"Open the path of communication. You might be surprised. I see the way he looks at you. Maybe he'll ask you to marry him and you won't need the job."

"Maria!" she protested, but the idea had its appeal. "You're jumping the gun. Besides, I still want to teach after I marry. No matter to whom or when I do."

Angela stretched. She felt drained and stiff. Memories of Ricardo's magic fingers easing her tension initiated ripples of longing.

A rustling noise from the next room alerted Angela. She looked up at Maria. "What was that?"

"Sounded like someone in the workroom." Maria headed toward the connecting door.

"Maria, what if someone heard what I said?"

"There's no one here." Maria stepped into the workroom and peered down the corridor that led to the offices. "And I don't see signs of anyone in the hall."

"Thank goodness. It must have been the air conditioner." Angela breathed a sigh of relief. "We'd better get back to our classrooms and finish our work."

"Why don't you go home early today? You look beat."

"Good idea," Angela agreed. "Would you lock up my room for me?"

"Sure thing, *mi amiga*. Get some rest."

"TAKE A LOOK AT THESE, Ken." Ricardo handed his cameraman the transcripts from Friday's session with Angela and the professors. "When you match them with the videos we've been watching, they bring the process into focus."

Ken perused the pages while Ricardo continued to view the monitor. Angela's beauty reached out to him. Her voice made him want to touch her. Again and soon.

He recalled the silky feel of her hair, the feminine fragrance that excited his senses and the satin texture of her skin.

"Sorry, what's that you said?" He ignored Ken's knowing smirk.

"I can see what you mean." Ken tapped the stack of papers grasped in his other hand. "Her methods make sense in combination with a voice-over explanation of the theory."

"She'll be happy to hear that," Ricardo commented. *She'll probably enjoy making me eat my words, too,* he thought to himself. He grinned, remembering her last method of revenge.

"What are you going to do with this stuff?" Ken looked up, not bothering to disguise his grin of amusement.

Ricardo cursed the close relationship that gave Ken too much insight into his thoughts. Most people were unable to penetrate the wall that covered his sensitive side. But Ken could. And now, Angela. The knowledge made him uneasy.

"I'm going to make it into a presentation of the whole-language theory. It'll be a good tool for Angela and the university staff."

"That's going to take some time. Can't imagine why you'd bother."

"Cut me some slack," Ricardo groaned as he quickly put his materials away. He glanced at his watch—it was close to three o'clock. Good. Maybe he'd surprise Angela and pick her up from school. It had been less than twenty-four hours since he'd been with her, but he wanted to see her again—now.

"I'm taking off," he told Ken. "Cover for me if something comes up."

"Tell Angela hi for me."

Just wait, he warned his friend in silence. The day would come when *he* would make an ass of himself over a woman. And then he would definitely know how love could threaten one's peace of mind.

Love. Where had that come from? Ricardo swerved the Ferrari into the left lane and made a U-turn. Maybe he should go home and let things cool between him and Angela. But he hadn't gone more than a block toward his house when he remembered the way her lips could make his blood sing. He slammed on the brakes and pulled into a parking lot. He swore, thankful that no cars were around to interfere with his erratic driving.

He headed toward the school and Angela. At the corner he stopped to buy a bouquet of flowers from the vendor.

Expecting to have to wait an hour, he was astonished to see Angela standing at the bus stop. With a loud squeal, he swerved to stop at her side.

"Fastest bus in town," he called out to her after giving her one of his best wolf whistles.

A smile began to tug at her lips and the dullness dimming her eyes began to fade away.

"What are you doing here?"

"Hop in and we'll go cruising." His heart raced when she climbed in beside him. "Why're you leaving early? Are you ill?"

"No." She shook her head, but he couldn't see her expression. Something was definitely bothering her. He would find out later when she wasn't so touchy.

Meanwhile the sleek lines of her long legs invited his hand. He reached out to trace the silky length of one nylon-clad limb. She showed little reaction.

She was obviously in a bad mood today. Maybe he'd done something to upset her. The thought worried him more than he wanted to admit, but he shrugged it aside and decided to flatter her out of her grumpiness.

Reaching behind her, he pulled out the bouquet of flowers. "Beautiful flowers for a beautiful lady."

Her eyes brightened for a moment, then dulled again. "I appreciate them, but it's no use. It's been a rotten day."

"Work?"

She nodded as her grip on the flowers crumpled the fragile buds.

Ricardo grimaced. At least this time he wasn't the cause of her bad mood. What she needed was some good news and some TLC.

"The results of the tapes look good," he told her. "I wanted to tell you about that. Shall we go for a drink and dinner?"

His words had the desired effect. He congratulated himself for the new alertness in her posture.

In the elevator taking them to the top of the Hyatt, he informed her of his findings. After the waiter seated them at a window table in the revolving dining room, he realized that her mood had lightened. He smiled in victory.

"I knew you would see how valuable this method is to those children." She beamed as she sipped on her glass of champagne.

"Here's to one of the best teachers I know," he toasted with a clink of their goblets.

Watching her over the rim of his glass, he admired her attractive poise. The sunshine filtering through the tinted windows made her skin look translucent. The expression on her face reflected dreamy contentment. Yet, he knew that earthy passion lurked under that surface sweetness.

He grasped the slender fingers of her hand and began to caress them. "You are a special teacher, don't you know that? You provide an atmosphere where children can explore and succeed."

He watched the glow in her eyes, brought on by his praise and so continued. "I saw in the tapes how their social interaction helped the children learn so much more. It isn't just your approach." He caressed the palm of her hand with his thumb. "It's your *cariño*, your love for humanity."

And love for him? he wondered. The word didn't alarm him anymore. He was sure of one thing: He needed Angela. And if that constituted love, then he wouldn't run from it. A strong urge to explore the depth of their relationship took control.

"Come to Sedona with me?" he asked. "We'll spend next weekend in luxury."

She stiffened and the joy fled from her eyes. "We can't do that."

Puzzled, Ricardo searched her features for a clue to her sudden wariness and withdrawal. Perhaps their rapid spiral of emotional involvement alarmed her, as well. He remembered his promise to go slow.

"Just think about it." He eased the pressure, wondering why she was hesitant.

"It isn't that I don't want to. I can't. I'll be in Tucson."

Ricardo stilled. He willed himself to remain calm. "Why are you going to Tucson?"

"Dr. Wheeler and I are presenting the whole-language theory at the State Bilingual Conference. We have presentations all day Thursday, and Friday morning."

The reprieve he felt was annoying.

"We were planning to come home late Friday night. The conference is over at noon but we figured we'd want to visit with some of our friends."

"Is Dr. Wheeler driving or are you?"

"You know me and driving."

"Do you think she would mind driving home alone?" Angela frowned and he went on to explain.

"I have to go to Nogales this week. Looks like they've busted a drug ring and my editor wants me to do a follow-up."

"You won't be at the board meeting tomorrow?"

"I'm planning on it. I don't leave until Wednesday, and I should be done in time to pick you up Friday at noon. We could leave from Tucson and head north."

"Sounds like a good idea. I'll pack a few extra things for Sedona and bring them with me."

"It's a date. And just in time. Here comes our dinner."

Their meal progressed peaceably enough, but Ricardo sensed that Angela was holding something back from him. It was nothing he could put his finger on, but her conversation was laced with an element of caution.

Finally, when the coffee was served, he decided to find out. "What happened today? You seem upset?"

She frowned. He wanted to erase the lines with his fingers.

"Is it something I can help you with?"

She shook her head and looked at her watch. "No. And I don't want to talk about it now. It'll spoil my lovely evening."

"I'm here for you. You can talk to me."

He could see the indecision in her expression, making him more curious than ever.

"Don't you have to get back to the station? You're on the air tonight, aren't you?"

"Yes, but I could come over afterward."

She placed her hand over his. It wasn't warm anymore but icy and damp. "That'll make it too late. I have to get up early for school. We'll talk this weekend when I have time."

He gently squeezed her fingers. "Promise?"

She nodded. "I'll tell you all about it."

Behind them, the setting sun turned the sky into an orange glow. It was time for him to take Angela home. He wanted to stay with her, but he knew she was right. They both had work tomorrow. Four days, and they would be in the resort town of Sedona with nothing to do but explore each other.

THE NIGHT OF THE BOARD meeting, the board members streamed into the conference room. With mixed emotions Angela watched each figure enter.

"Don't be so nervous," Maria chided her. "You said it wasn't set yet. Maybe they won't decide on an R.I.F."

"It's not that. It's Ricardo. He's coming tonight."

"So. I'd think that would take your mind off the R.I.F."

"It's because of the R.I.F. that I'm nervous about seeing him."

Maria frowned in puzzlement, so Angela explained. "He wants me to go to Sedona with him this weekend. I'm going to tell him I can't go."

"What has that to do with the R.I.F.?"

"Everything. Because of his influence with the board, I've decided to break things off between us. My past. It could be the kind of thing that would make them decide not to hire me."

"Ridiculous. These are the nineties. Besides, the R.I.F. is seniority-based only."

"You're sure?"

Maria nodded. "Don't ruin a good thing. And you can't knock a trip to Sedona. Go with him and have a ball. Your job would be worth it, not to mention that weekend in bed with de la Cruz...."

"Maria," Angela admonished her. Maria's ideas were too close to hers. What if she lost her job? A lump formed in her throat. It would devastate her, but she would survive. "I'm not going to Sedona," she swore with more conviction than she felt.

A sudden quiet fell throughout the room. Ricardo arrived and Angela's heart pounded at the sight of him. She couldn't deny the effect of his physical appeal.

Shoulders thrown back and head held high, he gave one the feeling that his strength could overwhelm you, and Angela knew it to be true. If he walked over to her this minute and said, "Let's forget the board meeting and go to my house," she would leave the room on the spot. She realized then that she could forget any noble idea about breaking off their relationship.

The members filed past her row of chairs and Angela held her breath. Ricardo came toward her and stopped. To keep from reaching out and touching him, she clenched her fists.

He gave her a cordial smile before sitting down in a seat across the aisle. No one in the crowded room would guess that they were lovers. She appreciated Ricardo's consideration but wondered how long she could keep up such a facade.

The board meeting proceeded but Angela barely heard a word. She tried to focus on the board members, on the superintendent, on Maria. But Ricardo drew her thoughts again and again. Her skin tingled and shivers raced along her spine.

Instead of school business, her mind filled with memories of their moments together. Were those moments more important than her job? Yes. She loved Ricardo de la Cruz.

After two hours, the board called a recess. Angela and Maria left the room, lining up for coffee in the lobby. Angela waited as Ricardo worked his way to her side.

Maria stiffened beside her. Angela looked over at her to see what was wrong. Cathy had stepped up beside Maria, who greeted her coolly.

"Nice to see you, Cathy. Did Lupe come with you?"

"No. She had plans."

Lupe and Cathy rarely came to board meetings. So why was Cathy at this one?

"You still going to Tucson?" Cathy asked.

"We're leaving Wednesday after school."

"So the kids will have a substitute teacher for two days?"

Angela nodded, wondering why Cathy was talking so loudly. It wasn't like her.

"Too bad. Subs are so hard on a class. They don't maintain the flow of your program. I'd think Administration would object to all the days you take off."

So that was it. Another of Cathy's attempts to annoy Angela. What unnerved her, though, was the public display. Why would Cathy overtly showcase her cattiness in front of so many people?

Angela kept her voice low as she replied, "My leave has been approved by the district office."

She didn't need this and decided to break off the conversation. From Maria's agitated shifting, she rec-

ognized her friend wasn't thrilled with it, either. She
sent Maria a knowing glance and together they tried to
slip away.

Fortunately Ricardo arrived. Angela didn't appreciate the way Cathy still was hanging around as if
wanting to eavesdrop.

"I thought she'd never call a break." Ricardo re-
ferred to the board president's action.

Angela could smell his after-shave when he stood
close. She forgot about Cathy and tried to keep up her
end of the casual talk.

"Will the meeting go on much longer?" she asked,
wishing her voice wasn't so breathy.

"Not too much longer. I came to tell you that they
want to call a closed session. Something came up this
afternoon they need to discuss."

"Oh." If it meant they could leave sooner, she was all
for it.

"Is Sedona still on?" he asked.

"Yes." How could she refuse when the smile he just
beamed at her was so devastating?

"Good. Let's go on in."

"I thought you said it was a closed session." She held
back, but he stopped and turned.

A strange look crossed his features. "The session
concerns you. They asked me to tell you."

"Me?" Angela stared, alarm racing through her. Her
heart was pounding, but this time not because of Ricardo's charm.

"And me. They requested we both be there. Strange
they didn't tell us sooner, but they said they just decided on it tonight."

She grasped his arm, stopping him. "What is it about?" What could they possibly want? Had they decided on the R.I.F. already?

"I don't know. We'd better go find out."

She turned to Maria, whose expression was sympathetic. Behind Maria stood Cathy, obviously curious about what was going on. Angela appreciated the protective way Ricardo was guiding her, his hand at her back. But it only served to increase her apprehension as they entered the boardroom and sat down.

The president greeted Angela and then, waving a letter in her hand, said, "We received this late this afternoon."

Angela took the letter.

"You understand," the president continued, "we don't approve of this kind of behavior from our staff."

In a state of shock, Angela stared at the letter:

Angela Stuart is having an affair with Ricardo de la Cruz.

12

"WHAT KIND OF LETTER is this?" Ricardo shouted as he stepped forward and tossed the paper on the table.

Angela stood in a state of shock as the board president waved the letter in Ricardo's face. "It's all here," she declared sternly.

"And you believe it?"

"Whether I believe it is not the point. The fact is this letter came to us. As far as we know, the accusation has gone no further. We prefer to keep it that way."

"Since when is it against board policy for a teacher to date?"

The president pressed her fingers to her forehead, obviously uncomfortable with this discussion. The other members of the board were clearly as distressed.

"Frankly, Ricardo, none of us cares to delve into this sort of personal information. But since you were a board member and are still actively involved in school affairs, and given Miss Stuart's background, we don't want to take chances that this won't blow up into a full-fledged scandal."

"What background are you talking about?"

"Never mind. I'll tell you later." Angela stepped forward and placed her hand on Ricardo's arm. It was bad enough to hear accusations. She didn't need her past dredged up, too. "What do you recommend we do?"

"We're not recommending anything. It will be up to you to make sure there are no grounds for a slandering attack."

"I resent the implication that we need to do anything," Ricardo said, his temper barely restrained. "Angela's and my private life are of no concern to you."

"I agree," the board president concurred. "But the fact remains, the report is here. Something needs to be done before you, Miss Stuart, and our school district are discredited in public."

"Don't worry." Ricardo strode over to Angela and grabbed her fingers. "Miss Stuart and I will get to the bottom of this."

Angela numbly followed Ricardo out of the adjourned meeting. She noticed the stares they received from stragglers outside the boardroom—not unexpected, given Ricardo's fierce expression.

Maria approached them and led them to her car. She unlocked the car doors and slipped into the driver's seat. Ricardo gripped Angela's elbow in a painful grasp, halting her before she entered the passenger side.

"I'll get to the bottom of this," he promised, unaware that he was hurting her.

Angela looked into his livid face and realized that Ricardo didn't regard this as unsolvable, and felt a glimmer of hope.

"What are you going to do?"

"I have some ideas. Remember, investigating rumors is my business. I'm good at it."

"How would anybody know we've been together? We haven't run into anyone from school, have we?"

"No, I'm sure of it."

"I can't believe anyone would report such rumors about me."

"I'll find out what's behind this, *querida.*"

His reassurance somewhat eased her anxiety.

"Can you come over?" she asked.

"No." He shook his head with regret and backed up a step. "I want to, but I have to head for Nogales. When I return I plan to do some research on these accusations."

His sinister tone sent chills down her spine. She let him seat her in Maria's car and watched as he went over to his Ferrari.

"What's going on?" Maria inquired while she started the engine of her sedan. "From the sounds of it, I would guess another war."

After telling Maria what had happened in the closed session, Angela asked, "Who would say such things about me?"

"How did Ricardo get interested in you in the first place?" Maria answered with another question.

"He heard rumors about my poor teaching methods— Oh, my God." Alarm settled across her features. "Someone's out to get me, Maria."

"Sounds like it. I wonder if Cathy and Lupe have anything to do with this."

"What makes you think they would? Those two would be the last I'd tell about my relationship with Ricardo."

"Remember the sound in the lounge yesterday?"

"They must have overheard me. But what would they have to gain by such viciousness?"

"You know they're jealous. You're successful and you work hard. That threatens them."

"We've gone over that. Surely by now they can see I'm not doing anything to upstage them."

"No. But your strategies work. They might be worried that they'll have to change their methods—or worse, work hard like you."

"It wouldn't hurt for them to put out more effort." Angela sniffed in disgust. "But I'm not pressuring anyone to adopt my methods. You can't force change like that."

"You're more astute than our administration. You know for a fact that if they see something that works, they'll try and make all of us do the same thing."

"But each of us has to teach our own way. Even those of us in the same whole-language program teach differently."

"Hey, you don't have to convince me."

"Sorry. This has me so upset I'm attacking my friends."

"Just remember that I *am* your friend." Maria pulled her car into the circular drive in front of Angela's apartment complex. "And so is Ricardo, judging by his defense of you tonight."

"I can see that now." Angela leaned her head back against the headrest and sighed.

"Sometimes other emotions cloud our logic." Maria reached over and patted her friend's knee. "I know you're crazy in love with the guy. Just try to keep a level head."

"Advice is so easy to give." Angela cast Maria a rueful glance. She had been muddled since the day Ricardo walked into her classroom. Now she had the threat from her school board to be anxious over.

"I wish I didn't have to go to Tucson," she said. "I should be here, defending myself."

"Just go!" Maria said. "You have too much to contribute. The rest of the teaching profession needs to know what you've accomplished here."

"But who's going to believe it? When word gets out that I've been fired, no one will be interested in what I've done." Angela's throat constricted and tears threatened.

"Didn't you hear a word Ricardo said to you?" Maria chided. "He's the best investigative reporter in the city. He'll find out what's going on."

"But Lupe and Cathy—"

"Leave them to me," Maria interrupted. "While you're gone I'll do some checking around myself."

"Don't put yourself on the line." Teaching was all Maria had. She couldn't afford to lose her job, having no family and no other means of support. While it would devastate Angela, she had her parents to rely on until she got back on her feet.

"Don't worry about me. I'm tough."

"You are. But seriously, don't let them find out what you're doing."

"It's late. Get out of here," Maria huffed, obviously embarrassed by Angela's concern. "You have a big day tomorrow."

Angela sighed. There didn't appear to be more she could say or do. "I'll go. Thanks for the ride."

"Go get 'em, and good luck."

"Remember what I said," Angela called out before her friend rolled up the window and drove into the night.

The phone was ringing inside her apartment as Angela arrived at the door. She scrambled in her purse, her anxiety making her fingers clumsy. It might be Ricardo, and she didn't want to miss his call. Finally she found her key and unlocked the door.

"Hello," she answered, breathless and worried.

"You all right?" The concern in Ricardo's voice immediately soothed her nerves. Thank goodness she had opened the door in time.

"I couldn't find my keys," she explained. "I thought you'd be on the road to Nogales."

"I had to stop by the station to take care of some last-minute details. I'll be on my way as soon as I hang up, but first let me give you Ken's number. I'll be in touch with him, so call him if you find out anything or need me."

Angela wrote down the number.

"Also, I need to ask you a couple of questions," he said, unnecessarily rationalizing his call. Angela would have welcomed his voice if he'd had nothing to say. "I want you to think back on all of your dealings with the university. Would anyone there want to sabotage your project for political reasons?"

His question astounded her. She knew from talking to the professors that competition existed for financial support of projects among the university staff, but she doubted they would involve her.

"I'll think about it," she promised. She couldn't afford to discount every possible factor. "I'll be with them for the rest of this week and will do some probing."

"And Sedona—are you still planning to go?"

"Do you think it's wise? Maybe we shouldn't."

"We'll be less likely to be seen together in Sedona than around here."

"True, but I don't like to think we have to sneak around."

"We're not sneaking around. We need to talk this whole thing through. It'll be easier if we get away from here and have some privacy. Don't you agree?"

"Yes," she admitted. "I'll be finished Friday afternoon, in time to go."

"Angela—I . . ." He started to speak and then hesitated.

She held her breath. Did he have second thoughts and plan to cancel their weekend, after all?

"Later," he finally said in a husky voice. "We'll talk this weekend. I have something I need to tell you."

What did he have to tell her? Afraid he might be ready to hang up, Angela stalled him, longing to continue hearing his voice.

"Maria and I did think of another possibility for tonight's fiasco."

"Oh?"

She explained about Lupe and Cathy, and Maria's speculation that the two teachers might be acting out of jealousy. Angela still found that inconceivable, but all possibilities had to be considered.

"That's another lead to look into," he told her. "Keep thinking like that—any small clue. You never know where it will lead us."

"Do you think it's as preconceived as that?" she asked him. The fact that anyone wanted to discredit her still seemed unbelievable.

"We'll check out every possibility," he promised.

His reassurance eased some of her anxiety. They talked for a few more minutes about nothing in particular. Angela had the feeling he didn't want the conversation to end any more than she did. The knowledge heartened her.

"DID YOU FIND OUT anything about those two teachers?" Ricardo looked up from his notes as Ken came into
his cubicle of office space. With frustration he rubbed
his fingers across his forehead. He was tired. He'd investigated the story in Nogales in record time and then
driven back Wednesday night. Two late nights in a row,
the long drive and the worry about Angela were taking their toll.

"Maria helped me out. We didn't find much." Ken
tossed a single sheet of paper onto his desk. "These gals
aren't too active."

"Another dead end." In disgust, Ricardo rocked his
chair back on two legs.

"What did you discover at the university?"

"Plenty," Ricardo snorted as he brought down his
chair with a bang. "But none of it pertaining to Angela. We ought to do a story someday about the political intrigue that goes on over there."

Ken laughed. "And spoil everyone's belief in the pu-
rity of the ivory tower?"

"Yeah." Ricardo grinned, loving the idea. It was his
kind of story. But not now. A frown replaced his grin.

"You look tired," said Ken. "Why don't you ease up
a bit and get some rest? You've been working all day—
not to mention the long drive last night."

"I know." Ricardo rubbed the stubble of beard across
his chin. The Jacuzzi sounded good but worry over
Angela's situation took precedence. He had to find out
who had wanted to get to Angela.

Looking at his cameraman, he noticed the lines of
fatigue around Ken's eyes. "You look tired yourself."
Appreciation welled up for his friend. Ken didn't have
to work on the investigation, but he'd fallen under Angela's spell, too. He admired and wanted to help the

dedicated teacher. Plus, Ricardo had a suspicion that Ken hadn't minded the chance to see Maria again.

"Let's go have a beer," Ricardo suggested on impulse. He shoved back his chair and grabbed the paper Ken had brought to take with them.

"You buying?"

"You bet." Ricardo gave Ken a slap on the back.

As they headed out the door and down the block to a nearby bar, Ricardo eyed Ken. They had been through it all together, climbing through the ranks of the television news, exposing corruption with each investigative story.

They'd met in Los Angeles, but when Ricardo had accepted the offer to report for Channel Four in Phoenix, he'd demanded Ken be hired too. To his knowledge, the station had never regretted the decision. Both men had won awards in the course of their careers.

In fact it was their growing popularity that had prompted Ricardo's editor to recommend Ricardo not run again for the school board. His name was becoming too big and his stories too controversial for him to remain in public office.

Ricardo wanted to serve the community but had to make a choice about his course of action. Ken understood Ricardo's frustration about that decision. After seating themselves in their usual booth, Ken again demonstrated his astute understanding of his friend.

"There're some rumblings at the station about your personal involvement in this case," Ken said after taking a large swig of beer.

"I know." Ricardo sipped on the ice-cold brew. "You know my motto—You Can't Hide The Truth."

"Then there is definitely something personal going on between you?" Ken quirked a rusty red eyebrow.

"You might put it that way." Ricardo grinned wryly, knowing there was more to it than that. Unwilling to admit it, even to himself, he changed the subject. "So what did you find out about those two teachers?"

"They were hired the same day as Angela."

"What has that got to do with anything?" Ricardo sipped his beer. Maybe he could drown the disappointment. So far, they had found nothing and this angle didn't look any more promising.

"Maria thinks it has a lot to do with the letter. Did you know the district is considering an R.I.F.?"

"No. Since when?"

"The teachers were notified last Monday but I asked some questions in the district office. It's been under consideration for six weeks. After a notice from the Department of Education. Evidently Valley of the Sun isn't in compliance with certain regulations."

Ricardo knew about the noncompliance. He'd warned the board three years ago that their program would be coming up for evaluation. Obviously they hadn't followed his advice.

"So how does this affect Angela?"

"Lupe, Cathy and Angela are close to the cutoff line. Maybe they think they can bump off some of the competition and ensure their own place on the list."

"That's it." Ricardo slammed his fist on the table. For the first time since this ugly business had started, he felt as if he had a clue. "I think those letters I received sounded too premeditated to be crank complaints about a teacher."

"What do you mean?" Ken asked, his curiosity aroused.

"Charges about a teacher don't usually come to a board member. They go to the administration." Ricardo began writing notes as he talked.

"So?"

"Angela's administration supports her; her test scores are high, parents like her; so why did *I* get the complaints?" Ricardo raked his fingers through his hair as he explained the letters that had spurred him into investigating Angela in the first place. "I thought they were in response to the special we aired. From parents. But they could have been a setup. This letter to the board was also designed to get her fired."

Ken finished his beer. "What are you going to do about it?"

"Nothing, yet. I'll check on a couple of other possibilities to be sure, and then Angela and I will confront Cathy and Lupe."

Ricardo stood and tossed some bills on the table. Now that he finally had direction, he was impatient to get moving.

"Whoever is threatening Angela—" Ken strode with Ricardo to the door "—I feel sorry for them. You aren't a man to cross."

"Don't waste your sympathy." Ricardo cast a menacing glare.

No one would hurt Angela. He'd see to that.

"YOU'RE SURE NO ONE on your staff has anything to gain by my being discredited?" Angela cast a hopeful glance at Dr. Wheeler as she sat on the other bed in her hotel room, her feet stretched out in front of her.

"There're plenty of professors who would gain from the whole-language program being abandoned, but I don't see how hurting you will do them any good. Attacking me or one of the others from the university is more their style."

"But my program proves your theories."

"Which is why you need to be your best for this presentation today. Forget the letter and pull yourself together."

"It's no use. I can't concentrate."

"Our presentation is in two hours." Exasperation etched Dr. Wheeler's voice as she encouraged Angela. "I want you to verify in your own words what results you've seen. Use the samples of the children's work you brought."

"I know what to say." Angela sighed. She didn't want to let the professors down. "I just can't get charged up for our presentation when I'm so worried about Ricardo and my job."

"He's more than capable of taking care of himself."

"But the damage to his reputation if that report goes out—"

"*His* reputation? What about *yours?*" Dr. Wheeler finally lost her patience and tossed her papers aside. "You're the one under attack here."

"But because of me, Ricardo and even the district could be harmed."

"Nonsense. A scandal would up his ratings. Besides, this has nothing to do with you at all. Maybe you're being used to get to Ricardo."

Angela's eyes widened as her statement sank in. Of course. Why hadn't she thought of it sooner? Someone had wanted to attack Ricardo. In his line of work he'd made plenty of enemies. Now she understood his explanation of why his editor had recommended he not run for the board a second term. Ricardo was becoming too big an item in the news.

"I must get in touch with him and warn him." She jumped up and began gathering papers, forgetting about her own situation, now that she thought Ricardo might be in trouble.

"Be sensible." Dr. Wheeler grabbed Angela's hands. "You're getting emotional here and losing your perspective."

She fought back her tears. "I love him," she gulped.

"I know." Dr. Wheeler sighed. "And you're letting that endanger your career, not to mention leaving us high and dry when we need you. Until this blows over, you're better off staying away from the man. That way, no one can use you to get at him. Nor harm you, either."

Angela's heart sank. Not see Ricardo? What about their weekend together? However, Dr. Wheeler had a point. If she continued this relationship, she and Ricardo would both lose.

"You're right," she admitted. "The best thing I can do is not see him until this is settled."

"And the conference? Are you still with us?"

She nodded.

"You rest for an hour," Dr. Wheeler ordered. "Think about what's at stake here. We're talking about revolutionizing the education system. We need your testimony. Remember your priorities."

Angela groaned as Dr. Wheeler left. She owed the professors so much. Too much to let them down like this.

She ran through the previous day's presentations. The educators who had attended their workshops had been impressed and eager for more information. The whole-language staff had a long road ahead of them to publicize and implement their holistic approach. At least work would help her to forget Ricardo.

Their weekend had to be called off. Resolved, she phoned Ken. "Will you be in touch with Ricardo this morning?"

"Sure. He just stepped out to do an errand before he heads for Tucson."

What was he doing in Phoenix already? Maybe he'd learned something.

"Tell him not to come down. We have to cancel the weekend." With a streak of uncharacteristic cowardice she added, "Tell him not to call me, either. We're through, Ken."

"Angela."

"Please, Ken. It's best for both of us. Will you tell him?"

"All right. But he's not going to like it. He'll be calling to hear for himself."

"Just tell him," she said before she hung up the phone.

So much for being a martyr. She felt awful. He probably would call, too. Maybe she should to to Nogales and spend the weekend shopping in the Mexican border town. The thought didn't lift her spirits, but she'd better get a grip—she had to finish the presentations.

How she managed the presentation that morning, she never knew. Showing off her students' work inspired her, as did the enthusiasm of her listeners. Dr. Wheeler was right. She must continue to fight for change in the educational system.

She placed another overhead projection on the screen. "When Carlos entered my class midyear, he was ashamed of his Spanish and refused to work." She went on to relate how Carlos's attitude and work had improved immeasurably during the course of the year. She glanced up at his poem on the screen, her heart swelling with pride at Carlos's accomplishments.

Turning to continue to address the crowd, she glanced around the packed conference room. Her throat tightened. *Ricardo*. He was here.

With effort, she concluded her speech, which received a loud round of applause.

While gathering her papers, she saw Ricardo approach. She had to physically force herself to stand still and not throw herself into his arms.

"Are you finished here?"

"This was my last presentation."

"Good. You're coming with me."

13

ANGELA JUST LOOKED at him in silence. He'd never ordered her like this before. He looked edgy and determined.

"Did Ken get ahold of you? I left a . . ."

"I got the message. Let's go."

Obviously he intended to ignore it. She had to make him understand a relationship could harm him. She loved him. She must explain how she felt before telling him to leave without her. "Come with me to my room." Her voice quavered with emotion. With shaky fingers she gathered her belongings before leading him upstairs.

After she opened her door, she expected the inquisition to begin. But not a word escaped his lips. He just stood, hands in the pleated pockets of his white linen pants.

He passed a cursory glance around the interior. Thank goodness she had packed everything away. It left the room neutral, with no personal sign of her exposed.

"I want to explain," she began while approaching him with hesitant steps.

He turned with sudden purpose. "Not here. Where're your bags?"

"They're packed and I'm ready to leave, so let's talk here," she insisted with more force than she felt. Part of her wished he would just walk away so she could avoid this confrontation. But the other part, the bigger part, wanted the consolation of his love.

Instead of responding, he opened her closet door, grabbed her suitcase and travel bag and headed for the door. "I'm parked illegally. Come on," he ordered with a toss of his head that brooked no argument.

"Where are we going? I told you I'm not going to Sedona."

"I'm not taking you to Sedona. You said you wanted to explain. We'll do it at my place." Impatience and a touch of defensiveness edged his tone.

"Your place. That's ridiculous. We don't need—"

He left the room before she finished. Quickly she followed him out the door.

"Let me leave a message for Dr. Wheeler." She veered toward the registration desk when they passed through the lobby.

"No." His curt demand halted her in her tracks. She turned incredulous eyes in his direction and saw his jaw clench in determination. "I already talked to her and told her you were coming with me."

"You presumed a lot." She placed her hands on her hips and glared at him. "She and I have plans to leave for Nogales in a couple of hours."

As soon as she had uttered the words, she realized her mistake.

His expression grew stormier. The muscle of his jaw twitched. "Don't say a word until we get to my place," he said, heading out of the hotel door.

Angela quickly followed. "I can't just walk out of here. I haven't paid my bill or—"

"You're checked out of your room." He tossed her bags into the trunk of the Ferrari.

Angela entered the car before he could assist her, waiting for him to sit beside her. She fumed. He had no right to treat her this way but she wasn't about to make a scene. People were already staring by the time they'd left the lobby. People she knew. This display wasn't going to help either one of them.

Ricardo climbed into the driver's seat. His temper matched hers. Probably surpassed it. She supposed he had a right to be angry with her. He wouldn't appreciate her decision to spend the weekend with Dr. Wheeler instead of him. She must make him understand why.

Ricardo drove out of the downtown congestion into the foothills of the resort city but then headed east instead of north toward Phoenix. He pulled the car up the drive leading to the Ventana Canyon Resort.

"I have a suite. We'll talk here," he explained in a gruff voice when he saw her questioning gaze.

Angela surveyed the plush surroundings while following Ricardo. Anyone she knew certainly wouldn't see her here. It was way out of her friends' price range. The inn blended with the rugged terrain. Huge windows allowed the visitor a full view of the city of Tucson below them, and crags covered with the majestic saguaro cacti towered behind them.

She followed Ricardo across the main pool and deck area and along a path to another level of buildings. Entering a small enclosed patio, Ricardo led her through the sliding-glass doors of a suite.

He had deposited her cases and turned to confront her. She stiffened in defense, forgetting all the reasons she had followed him here.

"Now, suppose you start telling me what the hell's going on." He cuffed his fists on his hips. "I don't like secondhand messages telling me to buzz off."

"I was afraid if I told you in person, you'd try to change my mind," she admitted.

"Damned right, I will." He scowled for a moment and then paced. "Why?"

Wanting to reach out to him, but not daring to, she grasped the full skirt of her silk dress with her damp hands.

"I refuse to be used to destroy you." Her resolve strengthened her voice so that it sounded deceptively calm and strong.

"Destroy me!" A stream of Spanish oaths rent the air.

When he paused for breath, she continued. "Don't you see? Somebody's using me to get you."

She had to make him realize that the accusations and rumors could discredit him.

"What makes you think that?"

"I talked to the professors." She licked her dry lips before explaining.

"They—they aren't involved in intrigue. I trust them."

"So you think someone is after me?"

"What else could it be?" She gripped the silk to keep from reaching out to touch him.

"It's not me, but you they're after."

"There's no reason. I'm nobody..." She stepped back in alarm when he stiffened.

"Don't ever say that again."

How could she walk away from that caring? It had to be now or she would never be able to leave him.

"I must go." She started to back away. "I love you too much to be party to any harm done to you."

What had she said? He stood between her and the glass entrance. Agitated, she turned and ran to the inside door, which she hoped led to the corridor. But her shaking fingers fumbled with the catch and she moaned with frustration as she heard him come up from behind.

"Angela," he cried out and pressed his body against hers, trapping her between him and the solid wood. "Don't leave, *querida*." She heard the agony in his voice.

She had lost her heart and soul to this man, and the knowledge calmed her.

Ricardo pressed his head into the curve of her neck. She had said she loved him. Those words kept echoing in his head.

An ugly fear had gripped him ever since he'd received the message that she wanted to sever their relationship. But he had only suspected the reason. Now that he knew for sure, relief and happiness surged through him—her reasons had nothing to do with him.

From the moment he had seen Angela, standing in front of her students, so proud of them and so enthused about her work, he had wanted her. Holding her now, he was filled with love.

He could feel her tremors and knew he should reassure her.

"You can't leave now. We have too much to settle." Slowly and carefully he turned her around to face him.

If she had hesitated or shown an inkling of doubt, he would have held back. But the yearning in her expression cut the last thread of his control. He lowered his head and pressed kisses on her mouth.

Angela's whole body trembled from desire and relief. How could she even have thought she'd be able to walk out that door? She'd told Ricardo she loved him, and she had meant it.

"Stay and talk to me," he whispered into her hair.

"We'll talk. But I don't want to right now."

He knew what she really wanted. He lifted her into his arms and carried her through the room. He eased her down and helped her to stand beside the large bed.

"Take me," she breathed against the pulsing skin of his neck. "Now, Ricardo. This minute."

"I want to make love with you more than anything, right now. But are you sure?"

"I need you."

"*Querida*," he whispered as he pulled her into his arms.

Finally, in a tangle of arms and legs, they ended up on the bed. In minutes they were both undressed. Their heavy breathing and moans accompanied the movements that in one moment would be slow and caressing and the next, lusty and energetic.

Too soon the wild tumble ended, leaving them drained and panting and entwined. The earthy musky scent of passion lingered in the air.

A long sigh escaped Angela's lips and Ricardo shifted his weight to his elbows and looked down into her face.

Her eyes opened—incredible eyes that seemed to reach the core of his being. A smile formed, warm and luxurious, that let him see the pleasure she felt.

"That was...mmm..." She trailed off in a lazy grin.

"It was fast." He hesitated. "Are you—"

"Lovely," she finished for him. "I feel delicious."

"You *are* delicious." He nipped tenderly at her lips. When she began to nibble back, Ricardo got hard.

"Witch," he murmured.

"Beast," she teased.

He admired her beauty. And she made him feel like a man.

He started to rise.

"Don't go. I love the feel of you."

He rolled over quickly, bringing her with him and nestling her head on his shoulder while he settled himself on his back. She molded herself to him.

"Lie still and rest," he advised her, contentment evident in his tone. "Next time, we'll take it slow and easy." He felt her smile when her lips curved against his chest. He closed his eyes, feeling utterly comfortable and satisfied.

For several moments they both reveled in the warmth and peace. But her earlier misgivings came back to haunt her.

"Ricardo. What about—"

"Shh. We'll talk about it later, after a bath and some food."

With a sigh, she conceded. It was all too easy to forget their problems in the security of his arms. Nobody was going to know they were together. Anyone from school who called would figure she'd stayed in Tucson with the professors. What was a couple more days? Time for love.

Angela curled against Ricardo's body, putting as much of her into contact with him as she could. Yes, now was time for love.

MUCH LATER, she purred as the jets from the whirlpool tub swirled around her body. "I'm hungry," she announced.

"You worked up an appetite making love all afternoon."

"I thought it was *your* hunger that needed satisfying."

Their voracious and wild lovemaking had satiated her. Since this weekend together was an unexpected pleasure, she relished every moment of it, planning to store up memories for the lonely nights ahead. And it was only Friday evening. With a flick of her hand, she sent a spray of water across his face. He grabbed her wrist.

"I could have *you* for dinner instead of steak or lobster."

"Don't you dare think of it," she joked, pulling out of his grasp. "We're eating real food before I fade away to nothing."

"We wouldn't want to ruin that sexy body. I'll order from room service."

"Good idea. I don't feel like getting dressed."

"How am I going to be able to eat if you're sitting at the table nude?"

Angela smiled mischievously. "I meant dressed up. But you have suggested an interesting idea."

"Why, you're just a big tease."

"*Quién*, me?" She reached for the sponge and began rubbing it over her skin.

His laughter vibrated across the steamy room.

"The way you mix Spanish and English makes me laugh," he explained.

"Thanks a lot," she said in mock annoyance. "All the studying I did, and you make fun of me."

"What prompted you to learn Spanish?" he asked while trailing his foot down the silky length of her legs.

"I told you. I traveled in Latin America." She sponged the other leg. "I was on a plane to San José, Costa Rica, and it crash-landed on a beach."

She paused.

"Why did your plane crash?"

"I didn't know. For two hours I tried to find out. But no one spoke English and my Spanish was so limited I didn't understand."

Her hands dropped in her lap as memories of the terrifying experience flooded her. In a hushed voice she explained how the customs authorities from San José had finally arrived to check them into their country. One of the officials spoke English and explained that San José was fogged in. The ancient aircraft had no flight instruments so they were forced to land on the beach.

"For that you learned Spanish?" Ricardo shook his head while he laughed in disbelief.

"I vowed never to be in that predicament again." Annoyed by his laughter and lack of understanding, she scooped up the sponge and dribbled water over his head. He grabbed her wrists but she continued. "It enables me to empathize with the students. I *know* how frightening it must be to enter a classroom of strangers and not understand a word or know what's happening."

"You don't say." He pulled her close and kissed her quick and hard before releasing her.

"Just like you must have felt your first day in my classroom," she teased while she splashed the sponge across her breasts.

He started to reply but her gesture captured his attention.

"Let me." He took the sponge from her and began rubbing her shoulders. She arched toward the soothing touch.

Love welled up inside Angela. She longed to know more about him, too; to be free to explore his past. Would there be a time for them?

"This tub is sinful, it's so big." She sat up to give him better access. The movement helped distract her from her disturbing thoughts.

"You're like satin." He placed kisses on the nape of her neck, while he slid his hands around her midriff to reach up and cup each breast. His wet, soapy fingers slid smoothly and silkily over the sensitive peaks and Angela gasped for breath.

Leaning back against the solid muscles of his chest, she closed her eyes, longing to tell him again of her love; but she dared not. He hadn't mentioned it and she refused to muddy their relationship with demands for words he could not and should not say at this time.

"If we're ever going to eat, we'd better get out of here." Strain made his tone husky and his fingers trembled as he eased her away.

Ricardo rushed out of the tub and grabbed a towel. Quickly he wrapped the terry cloth around her body.

"You could make a saint change his mind."

"You'd better cover yourself up, too." Angela cast an admiring glance at him. The way she could make him react with a simple look delighted her. She never guessed that a man could be so easy to please.

"Come here." He beckoned and preceded her into the bedroom after wrapping a towel around his waist. "I have a surprise for you."

The expression of excitement that brightened his features intrigued her more than the gift, but she tore at the blue bow and silver paper of the box.

She gasped in delight at the black satin teddy he'd chosen for her.

"It contrasts with your hair and your skin." He grasped the spaghetti straps of the teddy and held it up to her.

"It's so . . ." She hesitated as she eyed the intimate garment.

"Sexy." He said it for her.

To hide her uneasiness, Angela reached for the matching lace cover-up.

"I bought it for our trip to Sedona." He searched her face for her reaction.

She tried to smile but her lips trembled instead. "I don't know what to say."

"You don't like it?"

"It's lovely."

"Here, let me put it on." A quick flick of his fingers loosened the towel and it fell to her feet.

As he put the teddy on her, she searched his face for a clue to his feelings. Men gave their *lovers* gifts like this. Was that all she was to him?

Finishing his task, he glanced up into her eyes.

"What's wrong, *mi amor?* You look so sad."

She pressed against his hand. She wanted to ask, "Do you love me?" but instead smiled and said, "I'm sorry about Sedona."

"*Querida.* It's done. We'll go some other time."

His promise thrilled her until she remembered. Her smile faded before she spoke. "The reasons we didn't go are still there."

He cast her a puzzled glance and helped her into the lace cover-up. "What are you saying?"

"We have this weekend." She lowered her lashes, unable to meet his gaze. Rubbing her arms to ward off the chill inside, she continued. "After Sunday, we'll each go our own way until this is over."

"You're wrong." He placed his hands on her shoulders. Extending his thumbs, he lifted her chin. "Look at me."

She felt his power and confidence. With tremendous effort, she forced herself to remember her vow. "We can't—"

"Shh." He planted a kiss on her lips to hush her words.

Heat surged through her veins, making her forget everything but him.

"Don't you see I need you? I'm not letting you go."

Frightened of his ability to dissuade her, Angela pulled away from his grasp.

"Don't make it harder for me." She cast him a pleading look.

"I thought you loved me." He stood with legs apart and a determined expression on his face.

"Ricardo." Blood drained from her face. She should deny it. Her throat dry, she still tried to speak, but couldn't.

"Now are you saying that you don't?"

"No, no." Unable to bear lying to him, she threw herself into his arms. "I do love you."

She let the security she had always felt in his embrace surround her. She needed him, too. Would he ever speak the words of love she longed to hear?

Suddenly he broke away and began to pace. "You're right. This isn't going to work. We aren't going on like this."

Hearing Ricardo agree made her shiver with apprehension. It wasn't going to be easy to let him go.

"I'm glad you understand." She wasn't really, but she should be. "After what happened to me in Yuma, I couldn't bear to go through that again."

He paused at the sliding-glass door, his form framed by the desert scenery in the distance beyond. The light from outside was bright so she couldn't see his face. It was just as well. She didn't want to see his response to what she was about to tell him about that painful period in her life.

"What exactly did happen there? All I know is that you were fired. Didn't they understand your whole-language program?"

"I wasn't involved in the program until I came here. Losing my job had nothing to do with my teaching." Quickly she told him what had happened.

"Didn't you go to the board and protest? You had a good case to get that b—I mean, get him fired instead of you."

"Legally I had a case, but there was no way I was going to stay there and be the brunt of gossip. The other teachers didn't like me—which is understandable, now that I know the reason."

She had just wanted to get as far away from those miserable memories as possible.

"Do you want that to happen again? You love your job! You can't let this chase you away. We've got to fight it."

"No. I'm not going to be seen with you and risk our careers. Do you know what it's like to have people talk behind your back? I can't face it again."

"Your love isn't strong enough to fight for?"

"It's strong enough to sacrifice so that you aren't hurt," she insisted.

"I've got news for you. I'm going to fight for our relationship."

Relationship. Not love?

"You've ruled out the professors," he went on. "I've ruled out an attack on me."

"What else could it be?" She shook her head as her mind searched for clues. "I've never had any problems before this at school."

"The person who wrote the letter to the board is the same one who wrote letters to me discrediting you as a teacher. The type print matches."

Her mouth opened in disbelief. A nightmare. This had to be a ridiculous dream. Who would want to hurt her? "What did your letters say?"

"That you were incompetent, a lousy teacher, had no control over your classroom."

"You know I'm not."

"Of course not." He rubbed his fingers across his forehead. "That's why they want to get rid of you. Your success must be a threat to them."

She pounded her fists against the wall. Lupe and Cathy came to mind. The two teachers might be jealous, but surely they weren't malicious. "It doesn't make sense to attack a teacher who is doing well."

"Yes, it does." He stopped pacing and stood, arms crossed in anger. "Maria and Ken found out that Lupe and Cathy are close to you on the R.I.F. list. If you're out of the way, their names are closer to the top."

"That's absurd! One teacher off the list isn't going to make any difference."

"It could if you're on the drawing line."

"You don't suppose they've done this to others?"

"The letters I received were only about you. But who's to say they haven't found ways to attack other teachers?"

How politically naive she had been all these years. Ricardo would know what he was talking about, but

to destroy a good teacher's reputation was criminal. She
was livid.

"We must stop them. We can't let them destroy all the
work Maria and I have done."

"We'll stop them," he promised. "We're going to plan
a strategy this weekend—together."

"That's why you came?" She searched his face for
more.

"*Madre de Dios.* I couldn't let anything happen to
you."

Angela pressed her forehead against his chest. She
was glad he would fight by her side, but a part of her
ached with disappointment. She'd hoped his presence
here was for love, not just sympathy.

"I didn't want to tell you like this," he murmured, his
breath fanning strands of loose hair. "I wanted to tell
you later, on Sunday—after we'd had a chance to—"

"It's good to know now," she interrupted. At least she
would not make a bigger fool of herself by issuing more
words of love. They would only pressure him to commit, and he obviously didn't want to.

"But, come." He lifted her chin with the tip of his
finger and placed a light kiss on her forehead. "Let's put
it aside and order our dinner. We have time first for
pleasure."

She lowered her lashes, not wanting him to see how
his words hurt. What would they ever have together?
Physical delight and companionship were wonderful,
but Angela wanted more in a relationship. She wanted
commitment, love, and a lifetime together.

14

"DINNER WILL BE HERE in a few minutes." Ricardo turned, but his smile disappeared after he noticed her wounded look. "*Querida*, what's wrong?"

Cursing her inability to hide her feelings, she backed away from him and tried to maintain a cool detachment. "I think we should return to Phoenix."

"You're really shaken by this? I expected anger, but not the hurt."

How could she tell him that anger lingered, but that it was buried underneath a disappointment—a letdown caused by *him*, not by Lupe and Cathy's attack?

"Tell me you're going to help me fight." He lifted her face to his. His glance dared her to be strong.

Fortified by his courage and spirit, despite her underlying disappointment, she straightened.

"They won't do this to us. We'll stop them, Ricardo."

"I promise you, sweetheart." He kissed her with force.

Angela returned his kiss with passion. Desperation fired her hunger for more of Ricardo, and she demanded it.

Rough hands scoured her flesh with eager possessiveness and she reveled in his punishing caresses. His fingers slid under the lace cover-up and forced it to slither to the floor. Next came the thin straps of the satin teddy. The shimmery fabric caught at her waist as he lowered the thin straps down her arms. Trapped in silken fabric, she trembled with desire as he stroked her breasts. Straining at the straps that still constrained her, she moaned with need. Finally she struggled free and wrapped her arms around him.

An insistent knocking on the door brought them both back to earth with a crash. *Dinner!* Angela pushed away from Ricardo and grabbed for the fallen lace cover-up. Swearing under his breath, he quickly donned his black silk robe and left for the sitting room of the suite to answer the door.

Angela watched him leave while taking deep breaths to clear her head. One kiss, and she forgot everything. Trying to tell herself she should control herself, she rinsed her face in cool water. But looking in the mirror at the desire in her eyes, she knew it was useless.

Why not enjoy the weekend? she finally decided. She loved him. And that made it right.

Tantalizing odors drifted into the room, accompanied by the clink of crystal. As hunger pangs tugged at her stomach, it occurred to her how long it had been since she had eaten. One pleasure at a time, she told herself.

While Ricardo tipped the waiter, she quickly brushed her hair and applied a light coat of makeup. He rewarded her efforts with an admiring glance before he popped the cork of the champagne bottle.

Angela took one of the cool crystal flutes and brought it to her lips while maintaining eye contact with Ricardo.

Hiding the love she longed to show, she smiled seductively. "To our battle," she toasted.

"Our plan," he said, raising his glass to hers.

She sipped the tangy bubbles and lifted her goblet again. "To the weekend." Her tone held promise.

"To you."

ON THE AFTERNOON of the board meeting, Ricardo waited in front of the school, cursing his bad luck. Of all the times for the Copperville miners to stage another demonstration against the strike. Fortunately he'd been able to deal with his part of his plan for Angela before leaving on assignment. But Angela didn't know that. Furthermore, he had no clue how her role in the plot had gone. She must be frantic with worry.

How many days had it been since he'd seen her? Their weekend in Tucson seemed months ago. Several teachers entered and left the building before his hungry eyes focused on the one he most wanted to see.

Angela. *Madre mío.* She sent his blood pressure soaring. She walked toward him with that long-legged stride he loved so much. The full skirt of a dusty rose dress swirled with each step.

He stepped out of the car, wanting to gather her into his arms and kiss her senseless.

"You made it in time." She quickened her pace when she saw him standing outside the car.

"You bet." He smiled with assurance, unwilling to tell her he had moved heaven and hell to get here. "I'll take you to dinner while you update me on what happened."

"Did everything go well with you?"

"It's taken care of." He moved toward her, conscious of the scent of her perfume. His arms automatically stretched out for her, his need to touch was so much stronger than any concern for propriety.

"Is someone going to tell me what the hell's going on?" an irritated voice piped up behind Angela. Ricardo looked over her shoulder to see Maria.

"Maria and I were going out to eat before the board meeting." A flash of apology, quickly hidden, alerted him to her regret. "We didn't know if you'd be back."

"I was afraid if I stopped to call, I wouldn't make it." In spite of Maria's presence, he felt relieved that he had been here. Angela needed him now and her friend would be an added support.

"I'll take both of you to dinner, then. Two beautiful women—I'll be the envy of the crowd."

"Good. Are you going to tell me what's happening?" Maria asked.

When Angela cast him a questioning glance, he nodded his assent. "Sure thing." He chuckled. "The master plot is about to be revealed."

He squeezed Angela and Maria into his car. The tight fit didn't bother him and he suspected Angela didn't mind, either. Each time he shifted gears, he enjoyed the silky feel of her legs. With every turn of the steering wheel, his elbow pressed into the soft curves at his side. During the trip to the restaurant they exchanged glances of a private yearning. Damn, he wanted to kiss her.

Due to the early hour, the popular Spaghetti Company wasn't yet crowded. Ricardo escorted the two teachers into the restaurant and secured a table for the three of them.

"How did it go with Lupe and Cathy?" he asked after they were seated.

"They denied everything at first," Angela informed him. The look of distress that clouded her expression showed him how painful the confrontation had been.

She was too sensitive. "But I insisted I knew about their part in the scandal."

"So it was Lupe and Cathy who overheard us in the lounge?" Maria interrupted.

"Yes, and they admitted to writing the letters." Angela sighed in disgust.

"Did they say why?" Maria asked. "Was it the R.I.F.?"

Angela nodded.

"I knew there was more involved than professional spite," Maria said after sipping the wine Ricardo had ordered.

While salads were served with baskets of hot garlic bread, Angela told Maria what the two women had said.

"What are you going to do about it?" Maria asked. "Are you going to tell the board what they've done?"

"That won't do any good," Ricardo interjected, sounding calm and sure; but inside, his gut churned with impotent anger.

"Why not?" Maria brought him out of his dark reverie.

"We have other plans for them."

"And they're going along with them?" Maria's expression was disbelieving.

"I warned them that one wrong move—and I'll expose them." He couldn't help the ripple of pleasure at the thought.

"Ricardo!" Angela exclaimed. "What did you do?"

Their strategy had been subtle and manipulative. "Don't worry, *querida*," he assured her. "It's what we planned."

"Which was?" Maria reminded them of her ignorance in the matter.

"If the R.I.F. is enforced, they'll have jobs with La Causa por la Libertad."

Maria choked on her wine.

Ricardo empathized. He'd felt the same way when Angela had mentioned they try and find the women jobs in the local organization that conducted programs to teach English to adults, and provided job training and counseling for dropouts.

"Ricardo volunteers for the group and knows the director," Angela explained.

"Why don't you expose them now and get rid of them?" Maria asked.

"Because we need bilingual employees for the local organizations in the barrio to fight for important issues."

"Cathy's good at organizing. She'd be great at setting up programs," Angela inserted.

"And I have a feeling Lupe could handle the businessmen in Phoenix. La Causa needs a contact to solicit donations."

He directed his words to Maria but his eyes locked with Angela's. *Madre mío*, he would become a saint to keep receiving those kinds of looks from her.

Maria shook her head in disbelief. "And you're sure they'll follow through?"

"I'll be watching them like a hawk." Ricardo chuckled. "If they don't dedicate themselves to the job, they'll lose it."

"What if there's no R.I.F.? Surely they get better salaries teaching?"

Angela turned to answer her friend. He enjoyed watching her animated movements as she spoke; her lips so moist and inviting; her fingers waving in the air with suppleness; her hair shining in the chignon, begging to be released. He forced himself to focus on her words while he willed his tensed body to relax.

"I offered to work with them and show them my methods." Angela shrugged as she replied.

"You what?" Maria sputtered. "They deserve revenge—that's punishing yourself."

"I was tempted," Angela admitted, and Ricardo smiled to himself. He had wanted to punish at first, but Angela's sensitive nature insisted they change their tactics. Conceding to her wishes had been difficult, but he admired her for her stubborn reasoning. In the long run, their plan would benefit the barrio.

"How do you know they will do this?" Maria's skepticism resurfaced.

"If they don't—" Angela shrugged with a smug look on her face "—Ricardo and I turn in the evidence of their attempt to discredit me."

As Maria directed wide eyes on Angela, Ricardo watched Angela squirm in a slight bout of guilt for her blackmail. "Remember the alternative," he reminded her and knew it helped her to rationalize.

"The fact is," Angela asserted, "I think they're going to resign and take the jobs at La Causa anyway. You know they aren't that crazy about teaching. They'll probably enjoy working there."

"If they resign, then your job is secure."

"Exactly." Ricardo grinned. That hadn't been part of the plan, but as far as he was concerned it was the best part now. Angela belonged at the school.

"And the board? How are you getting them off your back?"

"Lupe typed another letter stating they'd been misinformed and they apologized for causing a disturbance."

"They signed it?"

"No. But the type matches. I plan to tell the board that we dealt with the matter and it's taken care of." Ricardo smiled. He also had other plans of his own, but they were to be a surprise.

"You both sound optimistic to me." Maria cast them a rueful glance.

Ricardo and Angela shared a secret smile. Yes, optimistic and positive—that's what he loved about her. He needed a woman with the insight to know how to brighten his life. Someone who would remind him of the positive things when he came home discouraged and depressed.

Heaping plates of spaghetti arrived and the conversation waned while they feasted on the savory food. In spite of the tempting flavors and famous recipe, none of them did justice to the meal. As the hour approached for the board meeting, all three grew tense and quiet.

"I'M SO NERVOUS," Angela admitted as the Ferrari approached the district office.

Ricardo reached out and patted her knee. She knew what Ricardo planned to say in her defense, but would the board accept the rationale? Had too much damage already been inflicted by the hints of scandal?

When they pulled into the parking lot, Angela glanced around in surprise. The place was packed with cars. Oh, no! Word must have gone out as to the subject of the closed session and the contents of the letter.

"Ricardo." She hesitated as panic set in. She tugged at the hand that he had extended to help her out of the car. "I can't go in there."

"I'll be at your side," he promised her.

"Great. Then they'll really have something to talk about." She moaned as apprehension tightened her throat.

"What are you afraid of?" Maria admonished her friend. "You have everything taken care of."

Angela took a deep breath to calm her nerves. If only they realized how much she dreaded public rejection. Calling upon all of her inner resources, she walked with composure between Ricardo and Maria. In the lobby of the district office, a crowd milled about. When Ricardo held the door for her and she entered, a dead silence fell throughout the room.

"*Señorita* Stuart!" a voice thick with Spanish accent shouted out.

Angela cringed against Ricardo as a cacophony erupted in the room. Her first instinct was to flee until she saw the familiar faces of the parents of her students—past and present. En masse, they surged around her.

"We came to help you."

"We tell them, you good teacher."

"They no fire you, *maestra*."

Words of support and encouragement deluged her. A lump formed in her throat, and tears ran down her cheeks as the impact of what these people were doing for her hit full force.

Touched beyond words, she turned to Ricardo and noticed admiration for her in his eyes. Her heart swelled with love for this man and these people.

"Did you do this?" she queried, and he shook his head in denial.

A shuffle at her side brought her attention to Maria. She saw the evasive smile and realized her friend had alerted the parents.

"Maria, thank you." She reached out and gave the teacher a gigantic hug.

She gave the parents a grateful smile and thanked them for their support.

"Come, let's go in. The meeting is about to begin," Ricardo said. They still had to convince the board that there was no basis for scandal.

Angela sat, numbed by emotion as each parent testified about her teaching, her loving *cariño* for the students and the generous help she offered their families. Mrs. Edwards spoke on her behalf and so did several of her colleagues. But the important witness, the person whose point of view mattered the most to her, waited until last to speak.

Ricardo's eloquence impressed the audience as much as it did her. It embarrassed her, though, when he made her sound like a heroine. But the crowd seemed to enjoy it, clapping and shouting their agreement.

Thinking back on his skeptical views of her teaching methods, she realized he had come a long way toward understanding her teaching methods. She was once again filled with respect and admiration for the man.

Watching him as he spoke—seeing the long fingers that could soothe her tension, and the broad shoulders so strong to lean on—she was overcome with longing. He planned to take her home tonight—he had promised. But what would happen next? And did he love her enough to commit himself for a lifetime?

Suddenly he stopped speaking and directed his gaze at her alone. She held her breath, sensing that this moment was important.

"I have one more point I'd like to clear up with this board." He spoke in deep tones to the members, but his eyes locked with hers. "With regard to the relationship between Miss Stuart and myself."

He paused and Angela held her breath. She couldn't believe her ears. He was bringing this up in an open session? A slight creak of a chair echoed in the silence of the room. Every pair of eyes focused on his words.

"I haven't asked her yet—" his voice was low and sincere "—but if she accepts, I plan to marry her."

Angela was thoroughly dazed as pandemonium broke loose around her. Her heart filled with overwhelming joy and it was all she could do to refrain from running to the podium and throwing herself into his arms.

She managed to nod in the affirmative, creating another wave of reaction from the crowd. But from that moment on, she had no idea how the rest of the meeting progressed.

Not until later, after accepting congratulations from her friends, calling her parents and finally escaping to the privacy of his patio, did they manage to say a word to each other.

"Come sit with me." He pulled her down on a double chaise lounge. "I want to tell you about your wedding present."

His arms felt safe and his body warm and familiar as she curled next to him on the comfortable recliner. She leaned back to look up at the stars, so faraway, and yet so near in the black night sky. A peace settled over her, the peace of feeling cherished.

"Remember the tape we made of your classroom?"

She nodded, but didn't really want to think about school anymore.

"I sent it to a friend of mine in Los Angeles. He produces documentaries for PBS. He's interested in making one on the whole-language approach."

"That's wonderful." She sat up in excitement.

He pulled her back into his arms and settled her head on his shoulder while he discussed the implications such a report would have on education. She listened—but more to the tone of his voice than to his words.

"He wants my input, and he wants to use some of the material we've already taped."

"So that's why you want marriage. You want to be sure I do this."

"Of course." He laughed as he nuzzled her neck.

She stilled his teasing with a kiss.

"Why do you really want to marry me?" she asked, wanting desperately to hear the words he hadn't yet uttered.

"Don't you know?"

"Ricardo."

"Did you mind that I put you on the spot like that in front of everyone?" He stalled as he caressed the smooth line of her jaw with his forefinger.

"I could hardly refuse with all those people there," she gently chided him.

"That was my purpose."

She sat up and searched his eyes. "Did you honestly have doubts?"

"I wasn't sure you'd want a man who gets called out at all hours for a story." He eased his fingers up her arms. "I'm out on assignment much of the time."

"Hmm." She decided a little rebuttal wouldn't hurt. "You have a point. Maybe I should reconsider."

"Don't tease about this."

"I love you," she told him, but she wasn't through with him yet. "Compromises are in order."

"Oh?"

"I can handle your absences if you can take the students I have visiting at our house when you return."

"Is that all?" He laughed before he kissed her and retorted, "They can play with *our* kids while you welcome me home."

Then Ricardo reached under the chaise with his free arm.

"I have another gift for you." He held out a rose made of blown glass, with petals that reflected like silver in the moonlight. "I love you, *querida*."

Angela took the rose and smiled.

*A magical three book mini-series from one of
Temptation's most popular authors*

GINA WILKINS

Three women, in business to create fairytale weddings for happy
couples. Follow all three as they each find the men of *their*
dreams.

TAKING A CHANCE ON LOVE

Chance Cassidy was hell-bent on saving his impulsive younger
brother from making the biggest mistake of his life – marriage.
But then he met the sexy wedding organiser, Liz Archer . . .

DESIGNS ON LOVE

Bridal-dress designer Devon Fleming was tired of being a "good
girl" and yearned for something more. Then daring foreign
correspondent Tristan Parrish stormed into her life . . .

AT LONG LAST

Holly Baldwin captured the special wedding moments with her
camera. But how did she set about capturing workaholic Neal
Archer?

Look out for these books available in December 1992, February
and April 1993. The most romantic of occasions captured for
your enjoyment in these special Temptation stories.

Price: £1.75

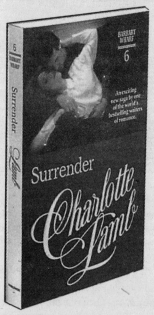

Temptations
and 2 gifts
yours FREE

Here's an invitation for you to treat yourself for FREE to all that's most daring and provocative in modern love stories, with 4 Temptations, a CUDDLY TEDDY and a special MYSTERY GIFT. And, if you choose, go on to enjoy 4 exciting Temptations, each month delivered direct to your door for just £1.75 each. Send the coupon below to: **Reader Service, FREEPOST, PO Box 236, Croydon, Surrey CR9 9EL.**

NO STAMP REQUIRED

Yes! Please rush me 4 free Temptations and 2 free gifts! Please also reserve me a Reader Service subscription. If I decide to subscribe I can look forward to receiving 4 Temptations each month for just £7.00 delivered direct to my door, postage and packing free, plus a free monthly Newsletter. If I choose not to subscribe I shall write to you within 10 days - I can keep the books and gifts whatever I decide. I may cancel or suspend my subscription at any time. I am over 18 years of age.

EP32T

Ms/Mrs/Miss/Mr _____

Address _____

_____

Postcode _____ Signature _____